Famous Fly Fishers

*Profiles of Eminent and Accomplished People
Who Love the Quiet Sport*

Norm Zeigler

This book is for
Libby, Travis and Katrina,
the loves of my life.

Acknowledgments

I would like to thank a number of people for their help, advice, and inspiration during the writing of this book. My fly fishing pal Dave Trout gets a pat on the back for his encouragement and companionship, from Sanibel Island to Newfoundland. Steve Brown gets a vote of thanks for introducing me to Norm Augustine. R.P. "Pete" Van Gytenbeek, gets a nod for his valuable personal insight about golfing legend Jack Nicklaus. Jerry Kustich, Dave Delisi, and Glenn Brackett at Sweetgrass Bamboo Fly Rods deserve another box of my mom's brownies for their hospitality and upbeat advice. Steve Bielenberg deserves thanks for his thoughtful suggestions. Bob Tully gets a "great fishing buddy" award for his enthusiastic support of the project and for sharing angling adventures from Germany to Oregon. I am also grateful for the support and positive comments – i.e., "neat idea," "sounds cool," "I'd really like to read that, etc." – from friends, fellow writers, and acquaintances who, without exception, were unstintingly upbeat about the book's concept. My publishers/editors at West River Publishing, Rick and Jerry Kustich, deserve the noble prize for their patience and professionalism throughout the manuscript's extended gestation period and their editorial and marketing expertise during the book's finalization. And, as always, I thank my loving wife, Libby Grimm, my best adviser and most steadfast advocate.

Yes, we'll gather at the river,
The beautiful, the beautiful river;
Gather with the saints at the river
That flows by the throne of God
—*"Shall we gather at the River?" Words & Music by
Robert Lowry, 1864*

And he shewed me a pure river of water of life, clear as
crystal, proceeding out of the throne of God and of the
Lamb—Revelation 22:1 (King James version)

Table of Contents

Prologue

There were two main criteria for choosing the subjects who make up this collection of profiles. One was that they not be professional fly fishing celebrities or fly fishing industry figures. The other was that the interviewees had achieved something noteworthy in their chosen callings.

It was a lot of fun to speak with and get to know -- at least tangentially -- the men and women whose stories comprise this book and I am grateful to them for sharing their thoughts, feelings, and especially their time. They are a diverse and fascinating group.

Some served classic American childhood angling apprenticeships, starting with stick, string, bobber, and worm and eventually matriculating to master status with bamboo or high modulus graphite rods tossing tiny bits of steel, feathers and fur. Some came straight to fly fishing as adults, finding on streams, lakes, and tropical flats momentary refuge from urban stress and demanding careers. They are politicians, jurists, businessmen, bankers, musicians, entrepreneurs, astronauts, scientists, academics, athletes, authors, entertainers, and artists. They make their homes in vastly dissimilar landscapes: by the surging sea, amid jagged peaks, and in throbbing megalopolises. They hold radically divergent political views. But they all share two signal traits. They have accomplished big things, things that set them apart from the madding crowd. And they love fly fishing; unabashedly and in the deepest recesses of their beings.

Chapter 1
Larry Csonka:
Football Legend, Alaska Devotee

When he talks about fly fishing, Larry Csonka's conversation is punctuated with self-deprecating humor about his skills, recounting his experiences in the kind of colorful vernacular heard around a campfire. "I'm still working on that (learning fly fishing)," he said, chuckling. "Anybody who tells you they've learned that, they're lying. . . . Take a close look at the backs of my ears. If I decided to wear jewelry on my ears, I'd never need anybody to pierce (them)." However, his is a modesty belied by scenes of great casts made and big fish hooked and landed on thousands of feet of film.

Zonk Productions

Csonka, one of the greatest running backs in the history of college and professional football, the heart of the offense on the Miami Dolphins' undefeated 1972 championship team, and a 1987 inductee into the Pro Football Hall of Fame, found his way to fly fishing through an early love of the outdoors. Born on Christmas Day 1946, he grew up hunting and fishing in and on the fields, streams, lakes, and forests of northeastern Ohio. It was a formative boyhood he recalled fondly.

"I hunted predominantly rabbits and pheasants. That's about it. Maybe a quail or two. And most of the fish I caught were either bluegill or bass, in northeastern Ohio. I caught 'em on every kind of cane pole you could imagine and every kind of willow stick you could think of. And any kind of yarn and horrendous rig that was possible I managed to get a fish with it," he said.

Later, at Syracuse University, where he was an all-American fullback, Csonka also began to pursue his advanced outdoor education. Alone and with friends -- especially Orangemen teammate Nick Kish -- he explored the nearby streams of the Adirondacks, learning to fly fish not by taking a class or finding a mentor but "just by doing it."

"There were planted trout in those rivers as well as natives," he remembered. "And there was quite a tournament there in the spring for rainbows. As far as fly fishing, you know you have fly fishing and fly fishing. I did a lot of drift the fly down the riffles . . . into the pool. But as far as placing and lofting and a great deal of disciplined directional casting . . . I didn't do that."

"I caught fish. I learned how to sneak up on a trout, how to lie down and see the surface, where the riffles were, figure out where the current was taking the bait -- the hatch -- by doing it. And to go downstream or upstream a little bit and inspect what was hatching or floating by and then try to match a fly to it. . . . And float it down from a distance, sometimes scrinching from behind bushes, much like a stalk on a pheasant feeding on the edge of a hedgerow. . . . And you learn not to walk heavy because vibration carries into a small stream."

In the Adirondacks region, he recalls, "There's a few brookies, mostly rainbows and I had a great time chasing them . . . everything from trolling with a canoe and drifting to trying to cast in under overhangs." Naturally, his fondest angling adventure memory from those years involved a big fish.

"I was there by myself lots of times, and just the fact I caught the fish tickled the fire out of me," he recalled. "I caught one in a stream up in the Adirondacks outside of Old Forge once that was a pretty good one. . . . For a guy that caught bluegills and bass it was a big fish."

"I had him up next to a glacial slide, a rock formation," he continued, "and I was fishing into pretty fast, deep water right off the edge of the cut, the rocks, and when I got him up there he was pretty tired, he was flailing against the rocks but I had no net. I hadn't taken the net over, I had left it on the other bank to wade across because the water was so rough to get over there, and I was on top of the rock pile and the water was pretty deep where I brought him up and as he was flailing around I saw that the fly was just barely in his lip."

"And I brought him up to the rocks and it pulled out, but he didn't know it, so I jumped in and pinned the rainbow against the rocks with my chest and started screaming wildly for my fishing partners who were downstream somewhere. I held him with me between my shirt and my vest and worked him along the edge of the rock until I got to a place where I could shove him up on the bank. And I piled out much like a cat on a mouse. And there were peals of laughter from my teammates and fishing mates at Syracuse who had been watching the whole scene from the other bank. But I got him, and took him home and ate him, that day in 1965."

Though he was a bruising competitor as a football player -- known for bulldozing defensive linemen to make big gains – Csonka's competitive fire never carried over to his time spent on the water. In 1980, after twelve stellar years as a pro, he walked away from the gridiron and its warrior mind set. Now, when he steps into a stream, he is following a more elemental drive: the yearning to be in and of the natural world. His relinquishing the attitude of athletic rivalry was one of the reasons he only half facetiously dismissed golf as "just a waste of great fishing time."

"When you play golf, what are you really playing for?" he asked, chuckling. "It just lays there. You knock it in the hole and then you do it again. . . . I just can't get excited about a little white ball. . . . I golf really well for three holes, then I'm just not worth a shit after that."

In contrast, he said, "When you can spot a fish, there's got to be no greater satisfaction in nature than when you take a spindly, 5-, 6-, 7-weight and you hook onto a four-pound-plus monster; with a fly that you presented. You know, like a really good rainbow or steel-head, particularly. You know how difficult steelhead can be, when she's lying in on her nest and she'll just lie there. It's like fishing a big, ugly, gangly fly for a mack (mackinaw, or lake trout) in the early spring in the Northwest Territories. You have to irritate her with that fly without spooking her. So your back is screaming and you're presenting the fly and on the seventy-first presentation you bounce it off the bank and snag it on a leaf and it drops with a little bit of green on it and you're thinking, ah, she'll never take that and that's when she comes off her nest and nails it. And all of a sudden you've got your hands full running up and down the riverbank trying to bring that steelhead in. . . . Tell me how it gets any better than that?"

As for friends and acquaintances who prefer golf to angling, "Some people hear the song, and other people don't," he said. "If you don't hear the song, you're not drawn to the outback."

The "outback" is his beloved Alaska, where at the time this chapter was written he was spending about seven months a year fishing, hunting, and filming his popular outdoor show, *North to Alaska*. The show chronicled outdoors pursuits in some of the wildest country for some of the most magnificent fish and big game animals on the planet.

Csonka gets a kick out of taking other people hunting for moose or caribou or bear but does not hunt big game much himself anymore. "I like to be out there, I like to watch the whole thing, and I like to watch somebody else's excitement," he says. "I've shot most of the game that Alaska has to offer at one time or another . . . and I don't have any more walls to put mounts on. . . . I don't have any real reason. I still eat caribou and, if I can get it, elk."

Instead of focusing on killing a grizzly or moose, on hunting trips he found himself constantly on the lookout for good water and big fish. "We always keep fly rods with us. We keep a 5, 6, 7. Sometimes we take all the way up to a 9 just in case we get into a saltwater tidal area and we get some big silvers," he said. It took him a while to catch on to the fact that in Alaska first-rate hunting and fishing often exist in the same places. He recounted one

"The first couple of years we did the show . . . I wasn't aware of the fact that I should keep a breakdown rod with me at all times. But having traveled around Alaska for twelve years now doing somewhere between thirteen and twenty-six episodes a year, I've learned . . . that there's always room for a breakdown rod and a small reel."

He told of one hunting trip near the Alaska National Wildlife Refuge that changed complexion quickly. "We got out of the boat and we were up on the ridge glassing for caribou and I kept a fly rod on the boat and I strung up a line and started fishing and I started catching dollys that were just unreal. Pretty soon, nobody's glassing, everybody's fishing. And we caught some lulus. We caught two -- twelve to fourteen -- out of there and cooked them along with our lunch."

Csonka loves all fly fishing, but one kind stands out for him. "As far as relaxing . . . just fartin' around and havin' a good time, I go out on a still lake in Alaska somewhere and I troll and I smoke a cigar. . . Next to being on a moose hunt or a fall bear hunt . . . it's probably the most enjoyment I get out of anything." He conceded that, because of the lack of action, it would not make a good episode for his show.

His favorite fishing area, he said, is the Anvik River and its tributary streams, which eventually merge into the Yukon. These extremely remote waters -- four hundred and fifty miles northwest of Anchorage – are renowned for big dolly vardens, grayling, arctic char, northern pike, sheefish and several species of salmon. But Csonka loves the region most for its wildness.

Though he is an Alaska resident, he maintains a home in Lisbon, Ohio. He also usually spends part of the winter in Florida, near the Indian River, where he fishes for redfish, snook, and seatrout. And when this was written he was considering a trip to Christmas Island for bonefish. But his heart is in Alaska.

It was a late January day when we talked and he was missing the far north. "I've been in Ohio for about two and a half months and I'm already starting to hear the sirens up in Alaska," he said. "I catch myself walking outside on these cold nights . . . and looking to the north to see if the (northern) lights are shining. I know they're showing over Fairbanks."

Csonka's best angling buddy is also one of his oldest friends – Kish from his days at Syracuse. In their early years fishing together, "We tracked a lot around the streams. Scared a lot of fish, we caught a few," he said. Still, as many of us have learned, no matter how much time you spend with someone on the water -- even over decades -- it is always possible to discover new things about him or her. The point was brought home to Csonka one winter when he called Kish to arrange a get-together. "I was trying to bring him some fish from Alaska and he says, 'I don't eat fish.' "

Csonka's eagerness to get back to wild country and big fish is a trait that one expects he will always have. And that many of us also share.

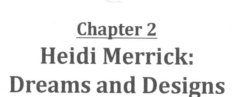

Chapter 2
Heidi Merrick:
Dreams and Designs

For fashion designer Heidi Merrick, life is a holistic circle of connections. And one of the most important elements in the loop is fly fishing.

Heidi Merrick

Merrick is a complex young woman: artist, craftswoman, businesswoman, nature lover, athlete, adventurer, and intellectual. In conversation, she exudes joie de vivre, punctuating her sentences and paragraphs with an infectious, uninhibited laugh. Especially when she talks about fly fishing, her tone turns philosophical and her words and speech patterns take on a wistful, lyric quality. And, in keeping with her Weltanschauung, she views her favorite pastime in broad overview and through a lens of interconnectedness.

For Merrick, the moments of accomplishment and inspiration fulfilled that come with creating a new dress or jacket equate to the magical, timeless moments of fly fishing. "I believe that it's almost the same moment on the river," she said. "I mean it's just a split second when you pull the fly up and you have the fish. And sometimes you have a great fight and a lot of times it's that moment when you catch the fish. You're just working toward that moment when you get the fish. Watching the water, watching the way the water flows."

Merrick's fashion career has followed a meteoric trajectory since she introduced her signature line of clothing in the fall of 2006. The Los Angeles Times has described her style as "California romantic . . . in bright sherbet-colored satins and chiffons."

She traces both her creativity and her love of fly fishing to her parents: her father, legendary surfboard designer Al Merrick, of Channel Islands Surfboards, in Santa Barbara, California, and her mother, Terry, a seamstress who sewed surfing shorts and Hawaiian style shirts. But it was her father who taught her to fly fish the year before she started high school.

"We used to do opening day of trout season for years," she said. But in those early days she used spinning gear. She laughed when recounting the "really funny story" of how she first came to pick up a fly rod. The impetus was what she remembers as the worst experience of her teenage years.

"I had gotten in a lot of trouble the night before," Merrick said. "I did something very bad." The upshot of her behavior the following morning was being wakened from a dead sleep at five a.m. by her furious mother.

"She ripped off the covers and said, 'You're going fly fishing with your father. I don't even want to see you,' " Merrick recalled. After being forced out of bed and into the car, she rode several hours with her father to a private ranch north of Mammoth. She did not know what to expect but was grateful that during the ride he never mentioned her transgression.

"He spent two weeks teaching me to fly fish," she said, and it was love at first cast. As a young girl growing up in Santa Barbara, she already led the active lifestyle of an avid surfer and gymnast. But fly fishing touched a different chord. "It really showed me a different way of life," she said. And in the intervening years (she was in her early thirties when this chapter was written), "It has calmed me down as a person."

One of the strongest threads linking Merrick's life pursuits is a sense of spirituality. She is perhaps one of the few people who can speak about it genuinely and unselfconsciously and have her words ring true.

She recalls a discussion with one of her company interns who reacted skeptically to one of her most axiomatic tenets: not to create any dresses that women would not wear to church.

"She said to me, 'What does religion have to do with fashion? . . . They're two different worlds,' " Merrick recalled. "I said, this is my line, this is my life. There are no lines between my worlds. This *is* my world. How can you separate them? When you're making a dress for my collection there's no separation."

The themes of spirituality and connectedness are reinforced by a quote from the New Testament she once displayed on her website, heidimerrick.com: "Put on a heart of compassion, kindness, humility, gentleness, and patience. . . . Above all these things put on love, which is the perfect bond of unity." -- Colossians 3

Other facets of her outlook on fly fishing include contemplative-ness and introspection. All of these components are closely linked to thoughts of the people she cares most about, the evanescence of the human condition, and especially the inevitable flow of time.

"I thought about the way my father is kind of at the end of his surfboard career, and longs to be -- you know, we have a cabin in Idaho -- and longs to be there fly fishing," Merrick said. "I was like . . . I wonder how many hours he spends staring at the ocean and the river and how they compare. And I thought, I bet that's almost his whole time, even though his career and his life are built on surf-ing, that he has spent almost equal time staring at the water and then I wondered what my time would be. Like at the end of our lives how many hours – I don't think it's a bad thing, I think it's a great thing. You know, when I stand before the Lord will he say, 'You spent nine thousand hours staring at the ocean, twenty thousand staring at the river? . . . I just wonder."

Though she does fish lakes, it is moving waters that capture her heart. "I prefer rivers," she said. "We have a cabin right on Henry's Lake (Idaho). That's where we go all the time. I don't really love fishing the lake as much as I do the rivers. My favorite is to float the Madison. I always pack a lunch and I love to get everybody in the boats. We also have two pontoons that we paddle, and I like to spend the whole day going down the river. . . . It usually ends up being nymph fishing just because there's obviously more nymphing than dry flying. But now I had Lasik so my vision's a lot better, and I've become a much better dry flier. My vision used to be bad and to me it was just . . . ridiculous." These days, missed strikes have become a rarity, she said, and dry fly fishing is "really much more fun."

Contemplating her favorite waters calls up a flood of memories. "When I was young we had a place in Mammoth so we used to go up and fish the Owens, and the Walker, and Rainbow Falls (on the Chehalis River in Washington)," she recalled. "I think we've been

11

fishing in Idaho-Montana since I was sixteen." Closest to her heart is the Madison, but, "I also like the Snake down from Island Park where it kind of rolls around," she said. "I've had some really good dry flying there. But I would say my favorite day is floating the Madison. Just because of the fishing at all levels. And we can have three generations there easily."

She regrets the time strictures that have, inevitably, come with her growing professional success. Beginning in her late teens, she has usually spent three weeks or a month at Henry's Lake. "The sad thing is, it's really different now," she said. She used to spend a month at the cabin in early fall, but now fashion interferes with fishing. "The tragedy is my New York markets are kind of the end of September and I'm at the point as a designer that I have to be in New York for Fashion Week. Which kind of messes up my fly fishing schedule," she continued, chuckling ruefully.

"That's one of the things maybe I was thinking about when I was wondering about the hours my father spends on the water and how many I would spend on the water," she continued. "Is at a certain point in your career, or a certain point as a wife and a designer, my time is not my own. And my father, who is the best in the world at what he does, I was thinking about how he gets away and takes his time and how it's portrayed by other people who desire his time, and wondering how I'm going to make time to be who I am in my life. And I think that's one of the things that I need to reconcile. And fly fishing is a really perfect example of it, because you really are . . . closing everything off to the world. You're spending days doing something for yourself, or just doing something by yourself, and I don't get that really right now, anymore. I have sometimes every hour scheduled for me." Merrick is eager to learn how other highly accomplished people who fly fish have "etched time out for themselves and how the people around them react to that."

Like all successful people, when Merrick dreams she dreams big. "One of my life goals is to have a house in Paris, you know, a fashion house," she says. "I've been working heavily on my French lately, and just I was . . . wondering . . . what European fly fishing would be. . . . One of my favorite books in the world is *The Sun Also Rises*. Some people might not make the cultural connection to city life and bohemian fashion and fly fishing but I think in *The Sun Also Rises* it's kind of quintessential to someone who was able to really love a city and live in a city and also someone will take three days to go fishing in Spain."

Her priorities go beyond financial success and fame and she understands that it is often the journey that is most important, not reaching the destination. "Something that was said to me when I was very young -- I don't think it has fully come to fruition -- but something that has tempered me and given me peace and a sense of direction is that . . . if all you fully look forward to is what you consider your success and that's all you're working for, afterward can come emptiness; if you do not have your joy and the strife of the work. And I think that's fly fishing. Fly fishing, you're often not catching fish. A very good percentage of the time you're trying and trying and trying to catch a fish. And that moment, those moments, as you change your fly for the fifth time, and you move down the river, as you take a walk . . . those moments are the real moments of fly fishing. And such as in life, the moments, my big moment the moment I'm alive the moment I'm living isn't when I show in Paris or when I show in New York. The moment when I'm living is my pattern work . . . in the studio, and my day to day making little deci-sions on the dresses, trying a dress four or five times, learning the fit of the body, changing the fit on the body, learning how to work and adjust to achieve my goal. And knowing that in those moments, that's my life. My life is not the accolades and all those affairs. It's really those moments when it's quiet and self-taught. It's almost like your instincts move you forward, you're learning and adjusting and honing your skills. And I think fly fishing and the practice of it really ingrains that in your nature."

There is no doubt where fly fishing ranks on her list of free-time activities. "It's the most intimate time for me. . . . it's my most coveted time and the one I really work to have. That's kind of the saddest part for me. . . . Honestly, the big issue is New York Fashion Week in September. . . . If I'm a designer I'm going to have fashion week at this time for the rest of my life. So, how do I work this out? How do I make it happen?"

She showed no hesitation in naming her favorite fishing companions: "For sure it's my father, and my best friend." She fondly recounted the story of how she brought her friend to the sport.

"The first time I took her down the Madison it was my father, my best friend Jennie (Murray Hooks), and my sister-in-law. And the river kind of split and we pulled off and there was a little caddis hatch. And we all got into the water and we put on dry flies and she had never fly fished. That was her first moment of fly fishing. We all put on dry flies and the caddis started really rising and we were catching a fish on every cast. We couldn't even see our flies there were so many. It was one of those moments where everything just converges. It may have been beginner's luck but I like to think it was just Providence, so she would be my lifelong fly fishing buddy. . . . It was by far my best fishing moment, because I had my dad, my best friend, and my sister-in-law, who I love with all my heart. She is the worst fly fisher in the world. She is the type of person who makes you take every fish off the hook for her. It is painful, and she catches fish. Which is so painful for me. She looks like she is throwing a lasso when she casts."

These days, Merrick looks to the future with the confidence of a woman living her dream in multiple permutations. "I've kind of reconciled the Santa Barbara surfer and the Montana fly fisher in me," she said, "so I get to participate in the world when I live here in Los Angeles or when I live in New York, or when I'll live in Paris. It helps me to swallow it a little bit and makes it romantic and wonderful for me."

Chapter 3
Harrison Schmitt:
Rockhound and Moon Rover

In his masterpiece novella *A River Runs Through It,* Norman Maclean wrote of the Big Blackfoot River flowing over "rocks from the basement of time." For Harrison Schmitt, geologist, Apollo astronaut, and the last of only twelve men to step onto the moon, the concept of time as told in the universe's ancient substrates – both literal and figurative -- has been the dominant theme of his life.

National Aeronautics and Space Administration

It was in the arid, mineral-rich landscape of the Southwest where Schmitt learned his distinctive world view from his father, a mining geologist who had moved from Minnesota to New Mexico. It would seem a problematic area to grow up fly fishing but, as many of us know, mountains and snowfall can create trout streams in seemingly unlikely places.

"I did a lot of fly fishing as a young person," Schmitt recalls. ". . . My father taught me, he was quite a fly fisherman, he grew up in Minnesota fishing the streams for smallmouth bass and he had a six-ounce rod, which I still have. It happens to be in Minnesota in the (family) cabin."

"We began by fishing on the Black River in . . . central Arizona. I also spent time fishing on Big Dry Creek in southwest New Mexico, which is a tributary of the Gila River down there."

A distant neighbor (they did not then know each other) of his growing up was fellow fly fisher and retired Supreme Court Justice Sandra Day O'Connor. "She was down there in what we call the boothills," Schmitt said. "Her family had a big ranch down there. South of where I grew up. Maybe fifty miles south."

Roughly retracing his father's career path, Schmitt earned a bachelor's degree in science from the California Institute of Technology, spent a year studying geology as a Fulbright scholar in Norway, and in 1964 was awarded a PhD in Geology from Harvard. In between his academic studies, he occasionally made time for fly fishing.

"Right out of college I fished in northern New Mexico, I fished the Chalmer River on weekends when I was working for the USGS (United States Geological Survey) up there. And then when I worked in the fifties up in Montana fished some of the tributaries of the Madison."

For Schmitt, fly fishing and other outdoor pursuits are a natural extension of his profession. "Geologists are almost invariably outdoorsmen if they're field geologists. It's hard not to be," he said.

"And I think that part of the profession, and professional geology as a whole, you have a pretty broad view of where they as individuals are within the universe are, where the earth is in the universe, and it is a combination of a view that has to make you somewhat humble because of the vastness of everything but yourself. But at the same time I find it absolutely inspiring that human kind has been able to do the things that it has in fulfilling its potential in terms of exploring the earth and now exploring the solar system. And ultimately who knows how far we'll go. That all fits into having this relationship, if you will, with nature, both the living nature and the nature of the past, which is geology."

He regards outdoor pursuits as more than mere pastimes. "I think fly fishing and all the outdoor activities that I undertake whether it's skiing or hiking are a combination of pure recreation to totally immerse yourself in something that you have to concentrate on or, in the case of fly fishing, you're going to put a hook in your neck or lose one up a tree. In addition to trying to figure out where those damn fish are. But the combination, particularly for young people . . . with learning how to take care of yourself out in nature is very, very important. It's not so much that you're taking care of yourself in nature, but you're learning to take care of yourself. You're learning to be innovative, to think through problems and solve them yourself. Unfortunately, people today don't get nearly enough of that, if they get any at all," he said.

In 1965, Schmitt was chosen from hundreds of other applicants as an astrogeologist for the National Aeronautic and Space Administration's Apollo moon program. He consulted and trained other astronauts about selecting moon landing sites and collecting lunar samples. In 1972, on the Apollo 17 mission, he landed and explored the moon's surface with Eugene Cernan for three days. They brought back two hundred and forty-nine pounds of moon materials for study.

While other lunar astronauts have described their experiences with reverent awe and in religious terms, Schmitt remains ever the detached scientist.

"Of course again, as a geologist, seeing the earth from the moon didn't surprise me," he said. "But it was a great opportunity, it was a beautiful place to be, and I'd love to do it again and I wish more people would have that opportunity." Though he is not religious in the classic sense, he does acknowledge a reverence for the mysteries of time and space, and humankind's place within the infinity of the universe: "Even scientists have taken some stuff on faith every once in a while."

Schmitt's outlook on science and religion ties in with his views about conservation and the environment: He is a strong proponent of so-called multiple-use policies and, unlike many avid fly fishers, an anti-preservationist. "I am a conservationist, no question about it," he insisted. "But I also grew up in the mining world, with my father being what we call an economic geologist. And I understand how dependent our civilization is on the resources that the earth can provide us. So balance is the important thing to remember, you have to have that balance necessary to make people's aspirations for a better life using the material resources of the earth while at the same time you conserve important areas so that they can be utilized for the more aesthetic aspirations of those same individuals, for the most part."

"Unfortunately, there are a lot of people in this country in particular now who think you can somehow have all the advantages of civilization without the materials required to support it," he said. "And I think had they had a more balanced upbringing if you will in terms of the importance of those materials and to their well-being at the same time as the importance of conservation we might all be a little better off and have less controversy about it. . . . It doesn't mean that you can't have conservation. There are major areas of the

United States and the world that *should* be conserved. And, particularly with modern technology, you can even produce resources from underneath those areas without any disturbance of any significance at all. But again, the politics of that have led a large number of people to think that somehow their civilization comes free."

"The role of fly fishing in that and other activities, I think it helps if it's combined with . . . a realistic view of what civilization's all about, that you develop that balance."

He also strongly supported the concept of user fees. "One of the big problems today is that we have set aside large areas that we want to preserve but we're unwilling to pay the price of managing those areas," Schmitt said. "Even though some of them seem quite large we have seen again and again, like those fires in Yellowstone and elsewhere, that unless you properly manage these they can destroy themselves, because they're too small to rejuvenate very rapidly."

"We ought to figure out a better way to fund the proper management of these areas. If you're going to have and perpetuate activities, like fly fishing or hiking in wilderness areas and things of that kind, bird sanctuaries, you've got to be willing to fund the proper management of those areas," he said. "Conservation of the resource. Trout, in a sense, are a resource . . . in the rivers. So they have to be conserved and managed if you're going to have them. But that comes with a price and I think the users should be the ones to pay that price. If somebody's not interested in fly fishing then I don't think they should have any obligation to the tax structure of the country to support it. Now I'm interested in fly fishing, so I'm more than happy to support it."

However, Schmitt does not want a Central European system, with fishing rights auctioned off to lessees responsible for maintaining fish populations and water quality. "My thinking is more along the U.S. model, where you do have national parks and forests but – there probably is some foundational support that is required out of the general revenues -- but for the most part if it is possible to do so I would charge user fees to the level necessary to support whatever that park or wilderness area requires. And those user fees can include some multiple use," he said.

Certain commercial activities, he maintained, can actually be beneficial. He cited grazing, with ranchers creating stock tanks on Bureau of Land Management land that help to control erosion. He strongly opposed a hands-off policy, giving as an example the failure to spray for spruce budworms. "If you really want to enjoy the benefits of wilderness, you're going to have to manage it. And part of management is to keep these insect infestations from occurring," he said. "It also hurts us in trout fishing, because if that happens in a watershed what formerly were nice trout streams erosion and that kind of thing is going to devastate the streams."

After leaving NASA in 1975, Schmitt was elected senator from New Mexico. On losing his Senate seat in 1982 he became a freelance consultant. These days, fly fishing for Schmitt is, like the rocks and minerals he has spent his life studying, mostly a thing of the past. "I've been too busy to . . . once I went to college, except for that experience in Montana, when I was working that summer (1958) for the USGS up there," he said. It is a situation he laments.

"And so, I've had a lot of fun with it but it's been a long time since I've had much contact. I've done a little fly fishing, trying to follow in my father's footsteps. Trying to get smallmouth bass up in Minnesota but I haven't been nearly as successful as he was."

"I still go up to Minnesota once in a while, we have a cabin on a lake. . . . But mostly I do plug casting and trolling. I haven't tried to use the fly rod in quite a while."

He would like to get back to his angling roots. And he knows where he will start. "I like trout; rainbow and brown trout fishing with dry flies, primarily. I spent a little time as a kid trying to learn how to tie flies but I've never caught anything on a fly that I have tied. But it was fun to try."

Occasionally he contemplates more exotic excursions: "I'd like to do some of the Scottish or Irish salmon streams, from an international perspective. But in the United States I would like to do more. . . . There are fantastic opportunities, of course, for fly fishing in Alaska and that's probably where I would like to do my next big search, in that area."

He wants to start again where he left off: by taking up his father's rod. "It's a six-ounce bamboo . . . the make of which escapes me right now," he said.

Chapter 4
Steve Burke:
NBC and MT

When NBC-Universal head Steve Burke was growing up, summer break and seashore were synonymous. "For me the summer was that if you had vacation time you'd go to the beach somewhere on the East Coast," he said. Year after year his parents took the family to Kennebunk, Maine, to sit in the sand and soak up the sun. He was not a happy camper.

"I get bored on the beach," he said. "I like being outside, but I don't like the pursuits that you have when you go to a place like Maine. I don't play golf, I didn't like sitting on the beach." But in the mid-1990s he experienced an epiphany on a dude ranch near Buffalo, Wyoming, that transformed his free-time focus.

Steve Burke

"I was riding horses for a couple days," he said, "and on the third day . . . my rear end hurt and I said is there anything else I can do here? And they said yeah, we've just started a program where we bring people on horseback with pack rods and we go up into the mountains and there's a stream up there and you can go fly fishing, but you need to learn how."

"So I said I'd love to learn how and I had an hour lesson and got on a horse and went up and the first day I did it I knew that I wanted to do it again and again."

"What happened was I recall I fished the first day and then I asked the guy if we could go someplace else the second day and basically for the rest of the one-week trip at the dude ranch I fished four or five days." When he returned home he knew he had found a new favorite pastime.

"I was living in Philadelphia," he said, "and I talked to some of the people I worked with. I said I really enjoy this sport and one of them said well I know there's a club in the Poconos that you could join. And so I ended up joining a club in the Poconos which had four miles (of river) and they would stock it with a bunch of trout and I really kind of taught myself the fundamentals of fly fishing."

"I bought a couple of books and I would go up and really didn't have that much help. But in a way it was kind of learning the hard way. I made a lot of mistakes and when I got better at it I appreciated it. I was fishing in the Poconos for maybe two or three years and then went out to Montana and fell in love with Montana."

Burke's instant affinity and passion for the sport surprised even him. But after a conversation with his father in which he learned a bit more about his family heritage the pieces of the puzzle fell into place.

"Very interesting thing, maybe eight or ten years ago . . . I told my dad about how much fun I was having fly fishing and he said, 'Well you know your grandfather, who passed away when I was very young, tied his own flies.' They lived in Rutland, Vermont. And he apparently was a huge fly fisherman and my dad said he gave a lot of his flies to my dad and my dad wasn't a fisherman so I don't know where they are. But I do think that whatever genetic wiring makes you love fly fishing was embedded in my grandfather and was embedded in me."

Burke eventually elevated his Montana infatuation to the next level with a commitment by buying a ranch near Ennis that included four miles along the Madison River at a series of braids called The Channels. Over the years it has become his haven and his second home. "That is my favorite place to fish in the world," he said. "It's great, it's wonderful."

Like many high-energy people, Burke leads a bifurcated life. "In some ways it's very different from what I do in the rest of my life, and I like that," Burke said of his fly fishing. "I am very, very happy when I am on vacation and spending ten hours in a trout stream, if I could. I typically go with my family and want to spend time with my family but to me, I could go ten hours by myself or with another person, not really talking very much. Every few hours talking about flies."

The other branch of his life is not so tranquil. "In my job I have lots and lots of people coming to me with issues and problems," he explained. "They need advice, or need me to make a decision and I kind of feel like people are tugging at my sleeve all day long and I love the idea of getting up in the morning and only thinking about catching fish."

"I love the solitude, I love the beauty of it. I feel, particularly when I'm in Montana, that I'm in a place that is spiritual and that I really connect to nature. I find that I get consumed by the fishing and it sort of takes my mind away from my day to day problems. If you're really concentrating on fishing I don't think there's room for much else to bring you back or weigh you down, and I love that."

"I like to cover a lot of ground, I walk a lot . . . . When I miss a fish . . . when my presentation isn't good or when I'm too fast to hook a fish, I get very upset. I'm a very intense fisherman and I think that allows me to get out of what I do during the day when I'm in my job."

However, despite the sport's escapist value for him, Burke does see similarities between the infotainment industry and fly fishing.

"I'm not the first person to say this, but the similarity of catching a fish on a dry fly is a lot like making a movie," he said. "When you make a movie you need a good script, you need a great director, you need great actors, you need the movie to be cinematically shot well. Then you need to edit well, and you need to release it on the right day, you have to have the right marketing. You've got to do about fifteen things right to have a hit film."

"And I've always thought that was analogous to fly fishing. To really catch a big, smart, wild brown trout you have to have the right fly, you have to have the right leader, you have to have a perfect presentation, you have to have a great cast, and set well, and then you've got to get the fish into the net. And anything can go wrong along the way. And I think that's what makes it so fun and so challenging."

Continuing the filmmaking analogy, Burke discussed an alternate scenario. "You know what, every once in a while you get lucky, don't do everything you should be doing, and the movie turns out a little differently than you thought and people like it and every once in a while you cast and it's not your best cast and you kind of know it but you catch a fish anyway. But by and large you have to do a lot of things right, which to me is why I like fly fishing, and ideally dry fly fishing."

He prefers the freewheeling advantages of wade fishing over boat angling. "I'll do a drift boat every once in a while," he said, "particularly if I have friends in town or I'm going to fish with my wife. Not that I don't like it, but I'm very independent when I fish. I really like to be by myself and move by myself. Even If I'm with a guide it's not uncommon for me to walk five miles just covering a lot of ground. I prefer that to being in a drift boat."

Burke has turned the fact that his job is bicoastal -- New York and Los Angeles – into a plus for his fly fishing opportunities. "I always take two weeks off, the last two weeks in August, but I go to Los Angeles a lot and I've convinced myself and the people that I work with that Montana's on the way home from Los Angeles. . . . Many times I'll work Thursday or Friday in Los Angeles, in June or July, and then on the way home stop in Montana for a couple of days.

So I think if you add it all up I'm probably over twenty days a year. Which is a lot. But I don't play golf and I don't play tennis, and it's really what I do when I can, when I'm not working."

Because his corporate responsibilities never take vacations, Burke has to stay in touch with the office even during his Montana forays. "I might spend an hour or two on the phone because the office opens earlier, because it's a two-hour time difference," he said. "But when I'm on the water I don't, I try not to bring a cell phone or a Blackberry. And I'm there to fish."

Since falling in love with fly fishing, Burke said, he has become "much more of a conservationist." One example is that he put much of his Montana property under a conservation easement. He also notes other side benefits far afield from his professional interactions with top broadcast journalists and the Hollywood glitterati.

"I've met a lot of people that I really like and really have an appreciation for cowboys and stream biologists and guides and other people that I've met in Montana and actually look forward to spending time with them and not people from New York or L.A. who are in the entertainment business. It's a very welcome change," he said.

Fly fishing has a positive effect on nearly everyone, Burke said, because "it rewards characteristics that are good to have. You're always trying to get better. . . . You know, there were days when I was five years into it when if I had a bad day it would bother me and I'd take the bad day home. And I think I'm a little bit more philosophical about it. Knowing there are good days and bad days. I've had some of the best conversations I've ever had with other people after a day's fishing. I think it puts you in a state of mind where you're relaxed and more open. I'm not sure it transforms me as a person but I think it certainly brings out good qualities in people."

Still, he emphasized, "that's not why I do it. I do it because I love it. It's really the only outside pursuit that I have that I just can't seem to get enough of. . . . It's definitely my number one leisure pursuit."

In contrast, Burke has no interest in one of his longtime boyhood activities. "I grew up on a golf course and I caddied for six or seven years in high school and when I was home from college," he said. "And I got to be a pretty good golfer when I was young." In recent years he and his family joined a country club in Philadelphia, where his wife and my eldest son occasionally play, but he underscored the fact that "it just holds absolutely no appeal to me."

He acknowledged that his is a minority opinion in the news and entertainment business: "I think in the media industry if you had a hundred people in a room and you asked those hundred people what they do on weekends the vast majority would say they play golf. There'd be three guys over in the corner who'd say they fly fish. And those would be the three guys I'd want to talk to."

It seemed natural that Burke's two best fishing buddies – Bob Burch, CEO of UgMO Technologies, a water conservation company, and Richard Beattie, chairman of a top New York law firm -- would be success-driven individuals like himself. Beattie, he said, "has a place in Montana near mine. But Bob Burch would be my number one fishing companion."

Burke reveled in the fact that he was still in his early fly fishing years and eagerly anticipated broadening his angling horizons. "I'm very lucky in the sense in looking forward to the future," he said. "I've never been to New Zealand, I've never been to Alaska."

When we spoke he was also pondering "a way to get my kids and my wife as hooked on fly fishing as I am. And I'm having mixed success. I don't have any of my kids who have fallen head over heels for it as I have."

"My theory is there's a gene, or some kind of genetic wiring that tends to happen when people who are a little bit Type A, and who are a little bit competitive with themselves, that makes them love fly fishing. And you either have it or you don't. . . . But I have not given up on my kids. And my wife is starting to enjoy it. I think I can see her becoming a really good fisherman."

One thing seemed certain: Burke already is.

Chapter 5
Kevin Richardson:
Whispering to Lions, Casting to Trout

Healthy skepticism, including a deeply ingrained distrust of the word "unique," informs a good writer's world view. But the life and accomplishments of South Africa's Kevin Richardson, known worldwide as The Lion Whisperer, are proof that the use of this literary pariah is sometimes warranted.

Kevin Richardson

Growing up in Johannesburg with a deep love of nature, and especially wild creatures, Richardson collected all manner of pets, from reptiles to birds, butterflies and mammals. That love eventually became a career and for more than a decade and a half he has conducted groundbreaking work with lions, gentling and bonding with them in an uncanny interspecies connection that is both admired and controversial. He first became famous at the Lion Park in Johannesburg and now works much of the time at his organization's facility, The Kingdom of the White Lion, about forty miles from the city.

Richardson's work with big cats, hyenas, and other predators includes conservation and management efforts throughout much of southern Africa, including his home country as well as Tanzania, Mozambique, Zimbabwe, Zambia, Namibia and Botswana. He is also on the board of the Protecting African Wildlife (PAW) Conservation Trust, which defines its mission as "committed to biodiversity conservation beyond borders."

As a self-taught animal behaviorist, Richardson is an iconoclast who admits to breaking "every safety rule known to humans" about working with wild predators. And like other highly accomplished people, the range of Richardson's interests within his chosen profession is contradictory. This was emphasized at the time this profile was written.

"I love all the predatory species," he said, "the ones that can really inflict damage and kill you. But by the same token, at the moment I'm raising a baby dove. Something that has always fascinated me as a child, you know, birds."

Though he declined to name a favorite species, it is obvious in his title and time apportionment that lions are at the top. He has cuddled and slept with them, kissed them, fed them and adapted himself to their needs, moods, and habits to become part of their "families." This is reflected in his autobiography, written with Tony Park: *Part of the Pride, My life Among the Big Cats of Africa.*

Thanks to the onetime global hegemony of the British Empire, which sought to transplant its favorite pastimes (i.e. cricket, polo, fly fishing) to many of the places it ruled, there is good trout fishing in Africa from Kilimanjaro to Capetown. Some of it is *very* good. (Other Brittania-created trout fishing destinations include New Zealand, Tasmania, Afghanistan, Pakistan and India.)

As is evident in conversing with a wide range of famous people, from authors to auto magnates and astronauts, there is no such thing as a stretch too large from profession to fly fishing. And, in fact, Richardson's love of "the quiet sport" seems like a natural segue, with the fact that both are practiced in wild places providing the logical link between his work and one of his favorite pastimes.

"It's a lovely way of just immersing yourself back in nature without having to think about all the on-goings of the world," he said. "It's amazing how quickly a day can transpire just by being in the wilderness tossing a line, even if I catch nothing the entire day. And you walk away from a day, walking in nature, in the wilderness, walking up these streams and you're coming back happy and rejuvenated. And people go, but I don't understand it, I don't understand how you can go five o'clock in the morning, and then be out the entire day without eating and come back in the evening and be happy."

Richardson was partly shamed into and partly challenged to take up fly fishing at seventeen by a girlfriend's brother in law. At the time a wild adolescent whose only angling experiences had been the South African tradition of "pop-coy" -- worm-dunking beer parties at municipal "dams" (reservoirs) -- Richardson took to heart his acquaintance's adjurations: "Well Kevin," the older man told him, "that's not fishing. Fishing is when you actually go out there and present the fly in such a way that the fish believes it's real and takes it." The words were enough to make him "quite fascinated by this whole thing called fly fishing."

At first, he admitted, it seemed a tough go. "I went with him to this place in South Africa called Dalstrom," Richardson remembered, "and, you know, snagged myself on the ear a number of times and caught nothing. And thought, this is a ridiculous sport, who would want to do this? You know, it was quite interesting, I got very frustrated and the line was snagging and was getting knotted and I thought this is crazy, people go out all day facing the elements trying to catch fish in this way. But you know, I got to get out a bit and I learned a bit about it and I learned to cast a bit better, and talked to people who were in the know. It's like most things, you start to enjoy it more and the more you enjoy it the more you want to do it."

When he met a man who owned a large piece of land in Dalstrom with "some amazing rivers that run through it" Richardson began to fly fish more and more and came into his own in the sport.

These days, he said, "One of my favorite places now is owned by an orthopedic surgeon friend of mine who's in his late sixties. So that's quite interesting, 'cause I call him a good friend and most people say, well he's old enough to be your father. So I say yup, me and him relate on the same level. He invites me to his place in an area of South Africa call Mpumalanga. And there's a place called Simsbury. . . . It's quite well known and it's quite a prestigious place to go fish. I thought, this is great because I'm in one of the hottest fishing places in South Africa by knowing this guy."

Richardson waxed nostalgic about Mpumalanga's rivers: "There's the Majiban and there's the Whiskey Sprite. If anything it's the most beautiful place you could imagine just spending time by yourself, even if you don't catch one single fish," he said. "And I get invited up there, a lot of the time I can't go because of work commitments and the animals. Whenever I get a gap I'll go and fish at his farm and just go out on the river and spend the entire day just fly fishing in the rivers. They've got the rainbow, and the brown trout is a little bit of a luxury. If you catch a brown you've done well.

So I have caught a brown there before and that will be like a wow!"

In explaining his affinity for the sport, Richardson drew a harsh contrast between fly fishing and his early fishing forays. "A lot of the fly fishers, in fact most of them, are in some way or another conservationists.... and very considerate kind of people toward nature and the wilderness around them," he said. "And that's one attribute I like. Whereas the other kind of fishing, where you just cast a line and leave it there, those guys are always drinking and drunk and the line's in the water and it's not about being in touch and in tune with nature. It's more about catching fish and having a fat jolly."

Like many a high-powered executive, Richardson also values the stress relieving aspect of the sport. "Fly fishing can be a social kind of thing, go away with two mates, we might not say two words to each other all day, but we've had a good time together," he observed. "And then I find fly fishing's a brilliant way of just being out there re-connecting. People think because I work with lions I'm in nature, and it's true, I'm in nature and I'm always in the wilderness, but it can become quite hectic because of all the demands. Sometimes I'm going to go out to these (fly fishing) areas and go into solitary mode, and go away from people for an entire day. And that's the best thing to recharge the batteries."

Still, at the time of this interview Richardson was beset by the same problem many highly accomplished people have – too little free time. "You know, when I was less busy than I am in the past three years," he said, "I used to go and fish six, maybe seven times a year. Nowadays if I'm lucky to get fishing once a year, it's a lot. . . . It's terrible."

He longs to visit a dear friend who immigrated to Australia; to fly fish with him in salt water, as well as for trout in Tasmania and New Zealand. And he looks to the future to take people up on the many fly fishing invitations he has received during travels around the world to promote his wildlife and conservation efforts. But, "Life just isn't conducive to that at the moment, unfortunately," he said.

"One day," he vowed, "when I get some time and I'm able to start fulfilling some other times I'm going to carefully look these people up and say, hey, remember me? Let's go fly fishing."

Still, he speaks lovingly of his calling and has no plans to cut back on the demands of his work with big cats to create more time for fly fishing. At the time of this interview he was working with thirty-one big cats at The Kingdom of the White Lion. He talked about "his" lions in a way that many people extol the virtues of, and express their love for, their children and, in the same vein, declined to pick a favorite. However, he does acknowledge special bonds.

"The first two lions I ever started working with are two male lions that are now turning fifteen years of age. Their names are Tau and Napoleon," he said. "And so they hold a very special place in my heart. And very close to them, following in a close second, is two female lions called Meg and Amy. And they are coming up nine, nine and a half. And the relationship there is also very special."

Like many highly motivated people, Richardson's cup runneth over with active pursuits, including flying planes and riding motorbikes. All of his favorite free-time activities share a common thread, he said: "No one can hassle you, no one can get to you, no one can disturb you."

For fly fishing he prefers dry flies and four- or five-weight rods and releases "ninety-nine point nine percent" of the fish. "There's very specific ways in which nowadays we catch the fish," he said. "You know, we don't bring them out of the water at all. Yeah, I don't even bring them out to weigh them anymore. I'm not interested in that, I don't care about the weight, I don't care about the size. I can tell people however big I want to tell them a fish was, you know? . . . I'm not taking a trophy and hanging it over my bar."

In recent years, he said, the face of fly fishing has changed in his home country. "Fly fishing has always been perceived as an old man's sport," Richardson said. "But, you know, lately in South Africa it's almost become trendy to take on fly fishing and you find a lot of these metrosexual men kind of getting out into nature with really expensive rods and really expensive reels. I think it's great because it's a way of getting people interested all their lives in getting out into the wilderness, even if they're not good fishermen. And suddenly you get these people who spent their entire lives are in the city, they're stock brokers or whatever they do, and they are appreciating nature. And that's the key."

Chapter 6
Norm Augustine:
Science, Service, and Far Horizons

It would be hard for anyone to find a man of more impressive and diversified accomplishments than Norm Augustine, former long-time CEO of Lockheed Martin. Augustine, a gentle bear of a man, extraordinarily self-effacing, congenial, and easy-going, acknowledges his feats and successes modestly and graciously. In addition to his science and industry bona fides – company head, aeronautical and rocket engineer, national defense technology expert, Army under secretary, National Academy of Sciences panel chairman – Augustine has also led a full and fascinating life outdoors. He has dog-sledded in Alaska, climbed and camped countless times in his

Norm Augustine

beloved Colorado Rockies, traversed the Boundary Waters Canoe Wilderness, and explored both the North and South Poles. And he has fly fished far and wide.

Growing up in Colorado, Augustine learned to fly fish from his father when he was around six years old. "My father taught me to fish," he said. "Dad had grown up in the mountains of Colorado in a little town called Buena Vista," he said, "and Dad loved to fish and Dad lived to be ninety-six. . . . Dad and I used to fish and it didn't much matter whether we caught fish or not, we just would be out in the streams."

"My Dad was really good," Augustine said. "He had moved to Buena Vista in 1896, when he was a baby, so he was kind of an outdoorsman. I don't think he ever took a lesson in his life, he just learned to fish by snagging willows and whatever else there was."

"That's where I really got into fly fishing. And when I grew up I left Colorado, I did a little bit of fishing in the ocean, bigger fish." But despite plying big waters far and wide, he said, "stream fishing is still my favorite, streams for rainbows."

"Although I love all kinds of fishing," Augustine continued, "I fish mostly streams in Colorado and Wyoming for browns and rainbow and cutthroat. I have fished for salmon up in Puget Sound and for tarpon down here (Sanibel Island, Florida, where he owns a vacation home) and for sailfish down in Baja California, for albacore off of California's coast and for whatever you catch off the East Coast, in the Atlantic. I'm not a lake fisherman particularly, I find lake fishing boring. I could never be a bass fisherman."

As we talked, Augustine sketched a modest and sometimes whimsical word portrait of himself in his own personal Bildungsroman. "Up until the time I left Colorado I thought the East Coast was Wichita, Kansas. I had lived a pretty limited life," he said, chuckling at his onetime provinciality. The limits began to stretch when he graduated from East Denver High School.

"When I was in high school in Denver nobody in my family had ever gone to college so it wasn't real clear what I would do, although my parents certainly encouraged me with education," he said. "So a teacher called me one day and asked me what I wanted to do and I told him I wanted to go into forestry and be a forest ranger. And he got a little bit upset with me and gave me two envelopes -- one was an application to Williams and one was an application to Princeton -- and told me to fill them out. I told him even if I got in I couldn't pay for it. And he said if you get in they'll pay your way, which they did. And so somewhere in the process of getting into Princeton they asked me what I wanted to study and I said forestry, which they thought was hilarious. They said we don't teach forestry, so I said what do you have that's like forestry? because I really like the outdoors. They said, well, geological engineering."

Augustine became an aeronautical engineer "by accident" when, after freshman year he met a casual acquaintance from high school who was an upper classman at Princeton on the train back to Denver. The man said he was majoring in aeronautical engineering and advised Augustine to change to the same discipline because it had "an unlimited future."

The change was one of the big turning points in his life. Augustine graduated magna cum laude from Princeton and stayed on to get a master's degree. "Sputnik went up the first year I was in graduate school and the new jets were coming out. . . . fall of 1957 was when Sputnik went up," he said. The United States began spending massively to win the Cold War and the space race and Augustine was right in the middle of it. With his exceptional scientific background and intuitive managerial skills he rose to become head of Martin-Marietta in California. When the merger came that created Lockheed Martin he was the logical pick to run one of the biggest defense and aerospace contractors.

His list of honors and awards includes the National Medal of

Technology, the Distinguished Service Medal, the National Academy of Science's Public Welfare Medal, and eighteen honorary degrees.

Considering the pressure cooker of his professional life, it is remarkable Augustine had any time for other activities. But somehow over the decades he found time to chair the Red Cross, head the American Institute of Aeronautics and Astronautics and the Boy Scouts, serve on numerous boards of directors, and become a trustee of Colonial Williamsburg. In addition to fulfilling numerous official obligations, he also indulged his love of the outdoors, snorkeling on the Great Barrier Reef, hiking, camping, and boating with friends and family and, of course, fly fishing.

Looking back on the busiest years, Augustine recognized that fly fishing was an indispensable relief valve. "It was an escape," he said. "I didn't think of it that way but I just enjoyed it so much. When you're standing on a stream holding a rod and a fly you forget everything else."

"I didn't get to fish as much as I would like, though," Augustine lamented. "Nobody ever gets to fish as much as they would like. But I was very disciplined about setting aside time. I kept a two-year calendar, so I would block time ahead for vacations. And I stuck with it pretty faithfully. I had a trick that I invented, which was if I wanted to take a week to do something two years from now I would schedule that week three different times, with the assumption that I would be able to salvage one of the weeks. You know, something would happen and I would have to give up one of the weeks. And something else would happen, but I was usually able to salvage at least one of the weeks."

"I enjoyed what I did, I loved the people I was around . . . I took a lot of satisfaction in my work, but that wasn't really what my life was about," he said.

When this chapter was written, Augustine and his wife, in addition to the Sanibel Island getaway, maintained homes in the

Washington, D.C., suburbs and, his favorite, at Estes Park in the High Rockies.

"Our front yard is Rocky Mountain National Park. Our backyard is Roosevelt National Forest" he said. "So people ask how much land we have and I say six million and five acres. Our place is at nine thousand feet exactly and it looks out on fourteen-thousand-foot peaks. We can see some glaciers out there. It's not very good fishing, frankly, it's better for hiking. . . . I love to camp. I've probably spent a year of my life in a tent. All added together."

A lifetime spent off and on among the high Colorado peaks has taught him important lessons. "I've been caught in lightning above timberline," he said. "I really watch the weather. . . . I remember one Fourth of July when we went out. In the morning it was probably sixty degrees and there wasn't a cloud in sight and by three in the afternoon the snow was coming down horizontally. That was up around eleven thousand feet."

"The high altitudes are so unforgiving. . . . We have a rule: You're off of the peaks by one in the afternoon and you're below timberline by two. And boy . . . I'm really rigid about that."

The Augustines' peripatetic home life contributes to family harmony, Augustine explained. "My wife is a beach person, I'm a mountain person. This is kind of a compromise. We spend part of the winter here (Sanibel Island) and part of the summer in Colorado and the rest in our Washington (Potomac, Maryland) home. If you can spend part of the time here, and part of the time in the nation's capital and part of the time in Colorado, how good does it get?" he asked.

Throughout his professional life a few activities did fall victim to time strictures. "I used to tie my own flies when I was young. . . and I don't know that I ever caught anything on them but my finger, but I had fun doing it," he said.

"With me, catching fish is terrific and challenging and fun but it's being in the out of doors," Augustine said. "I can come home happy if I don't get a bite. And that happened many a time. I think you learn from fly fishing and fishing. You certainly learn patience and you learn to relax, and you forget your troubles and things you're working on. I think it's just a wonderful, refreshing thing for people who live in a busy life."

After thinking long and hard, he could not pick a favorite fly fishing water. "I've fished in an awful lot of different rivers," he said, "but I suppose the upper parts of the Colorado I enjoy fishing, and the Arkansas. And the Frying Pan's a great river, and the Poudre. . . . I love to fish in the high country. That area (the wilderness near his Estes Park house) does have some fun fishing, but it's not like the Arkansas."

Early in his angling life Augustine learned a steadfast truism many of us plan by: "If you're willing to walk a mile you can cut out ninety percent of the fishermen and two miles gets you ninety nine percent."

As a younger man, Augustine also "loved" tennis and basketball. About the latter sport, he said, "I would rate myself a B-minus. I played basketball in the industrial leagues until I was close to forty." One suspects that this is excessive modesty, mostly from comparing himself to his son in law, a former NBA star.

His memories of the Boundary Waters trip – made with his now deceased son -- are sharp and poignant. "We spent a week," he said. "We started at Ely and went up over the Canadian border and camped. Boy that is beautiful country, too. We were there in August and at night you got a little bit of snow sometimes -- just a dusting. My son and I went up there and fished, just messed around. Again, I don't like lake fishing (they caught many smallmouths) and it didn't inspire me a lot, but the beauty made up for it."

At the time we talked, Augustine's time astream was diminished by his plethora of other interests. "I have so many hobbies, he explained, "but fly fishing would certainly be among the top ones. . . . I enjoy woodworking. . . . I love photography, which ties in with the outdoors, of course. I do a lot of animal photography.

"We spend a little time in Colorado at our place. And when we're up there I get to fish some," he said. When his children were young it had been otherwise. "My son in law and my son, particularly when they were college age, loved to fish. And they would get up at four in the morning to fish and you couldn't get them up at eight in the morning for anything else," he said, chuckling.

"I get out a little bit but I don't get out anywhere as much as I'd like. But I've got . . . two grandsons and I'm working on them. They enjoy catching fish."

Being an avid outdoorsman, including a fly fisher, has prompted Augustine's stance as a "pragmatic conservationist, in the sense I think it's nice for humans to use the parks, too," he said. "And I'm very worried about global warming, I think it's real and I think humans are probably contributing significantly to it. I just think how fortunate we are in this country. You take Rocky Mountain National Park, there's not a single signboard. And if we didn't have it, it would be today full of hotdog stands and T-shirt shops had it not been for Teddy Roosevelt, who had the foresight to set something like that apart."

After nearly eight decades of a multifaceted life filled with adventure and exotic travel, the powerful pull of far horizons had receded a bit. "I've been to the South Pole three times and the North Pole once," he explained. "I've traveled to a hundred and one countries. I took the trans-Siberian Railroad. Didn't get to fish there," he added, with a tinge of regret. "But I'm very content in Colorado. I can walk the same streams and find them different every time I go out." Still, he admitted, "I've not fished in South America. I've been invited a few times and I've not been able to go. I think South America would be a place I would really like to go."

He missed his best fishing buddy, Dick Seebass, a friend from Princeton who was the longtime dean of engineering at the University of Colorado who died a few years before. "There are just an awful lot of people I've enjoyed fishing with in my life. You don't meet bad people fishing. Most people who fish are pretty down to earth, salt of the earth kind of folk."

As to his favorite fish, he had no doubt. "Rainbow. . . . I like trout because they're in streams, they're good fighting fish, they're smart, and they're good to eat. What more could you ask?"

All three of his polar trips – two to the Antarctic and one to the Arctic – were at the behest of the U.S. government for scientific and military surveys. He described the North Pole as "Fifteen feet of saltwater ice with fourteen thousand feet of salt water under it. The South Pole is nine thousand feet of freshwater ice with land under it. . . . But there's not much fishing there."

One wonders when, or if, he will slow down, but idleness is not in Norm Augustine's DNA. At the time we spoke he was consulting for the Defense Department, the Department of Homeland Security, the National Institutes of Health, and the Department of Energy. His acknowledgement that myriad duties, obligations, and avocations can have a down side evoked a familiar refrain: "I really don't get a chance to fish as much as I'd like."

Chapter 7
Wade Boggs:
Baseball and Bonefish

Wade Boggs approaches fly fishing with the commitment and exactitude of purpose that made him one of Major League Baseball's greatest hitters. The Hall of Fame third baseman, who played most of his career with the Boston Red Sox, finished his Major League years with the Tampa Bay Devil Rays in 1999 with three thousand and ten hits and a cumulative batting average of .328.

Wade Boggs

On the occasion of Boggs' induction into the Hall of Fame in July 2005, Tampa Bay Tribune reporter Joe Henderson quoted Walter Woolf, manager of Boggs' Bayshore Little League team, the Royal Buick Wildcats: "I was the world's worst manager," Woolf said. "But even I could see how disciplined Wade was as a youngster. His father instilled such discipline in him that if Wade was the pitcher and a play was to first, he was always backing up the base. His range was the entire field."

Boston Globe reporter Dan Shaughnessy, in a feature also written about the Hall of Fame ceremony, quoted a later manager for Boggs, Joe Morgan of the Pawtucket Red Sox: "He had unbelievable dedication."

Boggs won five American League batting titles and appeared in twelve straight All Star games. He is described in his Hall of Fame thumbnail bio as "a virtuoso with a bat and one of the game's true masters at striking a baseball between the foul lines."

Boggs' toughness and dedication enabled him to persevere for six years slogging through the Red Sox's farm system, finally making it to the Big Show in April 1982. Boggs never got discouraged. Carter quoted him on his never-say-die attitude: "I was playing baseball," Boggs said. "That was my passion. You just have to wait for a break. That's what a lot of kids don't realize nowadays. They're just too anxious to wait for a break. They're sitting there going, 'Well, I should be in the big leagues.' Well, you're hitting .235 in Triple-A, dude. It's just not going to happen."

As sometimes happens, Boggs' good fortune came literally at the expense of another man's bad break. The Red Sox's previous third baseman, Carney Lansford, broke his ankle. The rest of the story, as they say, is baseball history. Boggs took over and tore up American League pitching for ten years with the Sox.

Boggs was not only a great professional athlete, but also a larger than life personality. Because of his personal idiosyncrasies and game-time rituals, Men's Fitness magazine named him one of the ten most superstitious athletes. Among the quirks of his playing years were: eating chicken before every game, fielding one hundred and seventeen ground balls in pre-game practice, waking up at the same time every day, and writing "Chai" (Hebrew for "life") – in the dirt of the batter's box during every at bat. When he won the World Series with the 1996 Yankees – he had left the Red Sox after a salary dispute in 1992 -- Boggs jumped on the back of a mounted patrol policeman's horse to parade around the stadium.

Born in Omaha, Nebraska, Boggs' early boyhood was spent in the peripatetic life of a military family (his father, Winn, was a World War II Marine, then an Air Force pilot). In 1969, two years after Winn's retirement from the military, the family moved to Tampa, Florida, where Boggs was a star athlete – playing both baseball and football – at H.B. Plant High School. He also grew up prospecting the fish-rich, subtropical waters of southwest Florida with his father and friends. For his first four decades, fishing meant spinning and conventional gear. That changed thanks to a thoughtful gift.

"My wife gave me a fly reel and a fly rod for my fortieth birthday," Boggs said. "I started quite a bit late in life as far as fly fishing goes. I wanted to get into the bonefishing with a fly down in the Bahamas and fly fishing for sailfish. She gave me an 8-weight for bonefish and a 14-weight for sailfish in Costa Rica."

Another crucial trait of both his baseball and fly fishing success is patience. As a ballplayer, Boggs was famous for his eagle eye for the strike zone and for showing Zen-like restraint while waiting for the right pitch to hit. He also showed long-term patience in both sports, toiling doggedly for those six years in the minor leagues after high school before being called up to the Red Sox, and prowling and casting for days on end for bonefish to perfect his angling skills. Like a lot of strong-willed people, he did most of his learning on his own.

"I'm more or less self taught," Boggs said. "Watched people throw on TV and did the double haul, and things of that nature. I never really had a lesson. You hope the eye-hand coordination can work out where you can master the double haul. The only way to do it is to go down to the Bahamas, walk the flats, and just keep trying. Basically that's what I did."

He did not gloss over the fact that he did not become an instant expert. "It took a lot of work and a lot of practice," Boggs said. "Maybe two years. And applying yourself." The rewards, he said, come on the "days when everything falls into place."

"For me fly fishing is something that was extremely difficult, and it's not for everybody, because you think the spinning reel or the bait caster or something like that, there's always one more. And I think that fly fishing is probably the pinnacle of all fishing. It's probably the last thing that people can learn, as far as fishing goes. It is extremely difficult but extremely rewarding."

The quarry and the place where he learned to cast a fly remain at the top of his favorites lists. He drew a sharp distinction between wading the Bahamas flats in search of bones and "being poled around in a boat in Florida. You're in the water, you're casting, at times you're knee deep, at times you're a mile or two miles away from the boat and carrying extra flies and all of this, and really sight fishing."

"When you get down in the Keys I'm sure that if you talk to any Florida guide down there he's got his favorite place in the Keys," Boggs continues, "but when you get into that pristine water in the Bahamas . . . and you get out of the boat and start walking . . . and can see a bonefish at about eighty yards and walking up it's just an unbelievable place. And the quantity of the bonefish that are down there, it's an easy place to learn. You're not going to be frustrated by having two or three shots in one day. . . . In the Bahamas you've got them swimming between your legs and it's multiple shots. It's a neat playground to learn on and at the end of the day you're rewarded by the efforts that you've put forth. It's not uncharacteristic to go down and catch anywhere from fifteen to twenty-five bonefish in a day just by walking the flats. And like I said, one or two shots in the Keys on a fly is a pretty good day."

Like many of us, including other subjects of this book, Boggs loves fly fishing for another reason: "It's a solitude sport, you have to have space. It's not like getting a spinning rod out with somebody standing next to you. You've definitely got to have space. It's more a solitary game than anything else."

As he did with baseball, Boggs keeps pushing himself to new accomplishments -- bigger fish, lighter leaders, more species.

"It's just pushing the envelope further," he said, giving as an example the next quest he had set for himself when we spoke: a hundred-pound tarpon. He spoke of the challenge with relish: "I've caught small, baby tarpon on fly, but nothing like over eighty into the hundred on a fly."

Like the home run he hit for his three thousandth hit, he is gratified by one personal fly fishing milestone. "An extreme accomplishment that I've felt is catching the sailfish on a fly in Costa Rica," he said. "And having the opportunity to bring one of those in. I've gone everywhere from seven minutes to two hours and forty-five minutes."

Talking with him, one gets the impression that Boggs regards the varying challenges of sailfishing as loosely analogous to those encountered facing different pitchers and pitches, playing in different ballparks and for different teams, and other baseball variables. "The discrepancy of how long it takes really depends not only on your captain but how the fish cooperates," he explained. "Sometimes it's a quick process, fifteen or twenty minutes, and sometimes the fish will sound under the boat, and it takes you in the neighborhood of two, two and a half hours. It's extremely difficult, but once you get him in the boat, take a picture and then know that you've gone away from the conventional style to catch a fish on a fly that's in the hundred and thirty, hundred and forty pound range, it's completely satisfying."

The fact that fly fishing is "right up at the top of the list" among his free-time pursuits, Boggs said, means that, "If I go anywhere where there's fishing, I carry a fly rod. . . . When I was elk hunting in Montana (several years before) we would get out on the (ranch) lake and fly fish for rainbows and various other trout."

New adventures beckoned. "I want to venture onto the marlin scene now," he said. "And, like I said, just keep coming up with ideas and various places to just keeping putting notches in that gun belt where you can say, yeah I've accomplished this with a fly, I've accomplished that," Boggs said. One destination was the Land of the Midnight Sun.

"I think that getting into the Alaska part of it, fly fishing for the big salmon and trout that they have there, that would be the next journey that I would like to accomplish," Boggs said. Also at the back of his mind was a dream trip for peacock bass in South America. Closer to home, he pursued snook and redfish in the waters around Tampa and St. Petersburg. Snook are among his favorites.

"We do it around the docks and things of that nature. A lot of times we'll get out at night and trying to fly fish at night is difficult but we do the lights around the docks. . . . Oh yeah, snook on a fly, absolutely."

Boggs has two close, longtime fishing buddies: his wife, Debbie, and his longtime friend T.J. Ferlita. "When we go to Costa Rica I go with my wife. And she has the opportunity to fish for the sailfish that I miss with the fly. She catches one on a spinning reel when he misses the fly. She picks up my slack," he said, chuckling.

With Ferlita, it is the continuation of a longtime friendship. "We go all the way back to the high school days," Boggs said. A few years back, "I got him fly fishing and going down to the Bahamas together."

At the time this chapter was written, Boggs was also fishing in many charity tournaments to benefit cystic fibrosis research.

Chapter 8
Christopher Parkening:
Faith, Fame, and Fly Fishing

For Christopher Parkening, one of the world's great classical gui-
tarists, life is comprised mainly of four crucial components: an abiding and powerful religious faith, a genius for music, love of family,
and a lifelong passion for fly fishing. These and other, more subtle,
character traits -- i.e., an adventurous spirit, innate tranquility, abiding
kindness -- make him one of the most remarkable public personalities.

Christopher Parkening

Talking with Parkening one is struck by his voice and manner, not strictly soft-spoken but mellifluous, almost musical, a speaking style marked by muted surface tones but submerging deep currents of thought and emotion. Thoughts and emotions that he imparts in his conversation and in his captivating autobiography, *Grace Like a River*. And, of course, in his music.

Parkening came to fly fishing early, learning from his father, Duke Parkening, at age six in their backyard in Los Angeles. In his early teens he and his father became friends with casting champion Jimmy Green, designer for Fenwick fly rods. They both spent many weekends at the legendary Long Beach Casting Club perfecting their techniques and broadening their knowledge for their main interest—fly fishing. Parkening even won the Western States All-Around Casting Championship at age 19.

Music also entered his life at six, when he started playing the ukulele. At eleven he began his serious musical quest, learning to play the classical guitar under a daunting and almost unheard of (for a young boy) practice schedule of an hour and a half at 5:30 a.m. each morning before school, again after he returned home, and five hours during the weekend. Although he enjoyed school team sports, the long hours devoted to his music precluded his pursuing most of them. However, his family and he always made time for one sport.

"My favorite sport ... one that has given me lifelong pleasure, was fly-fishing for trout," he wrote in *Grace Like a River*.

Hot Creek Ranch, a seven thousand foot-altitude, two hundred and twenty-acre spread bisected by a prolific spring creek was the family's favorite fly fishing destination during Parkening's early boyhood and teen years. Located amid the stunning peaks of the high Sierras and blessed with abundant insect life and many large fish, the stream was the stuff of dry fly fishers' dreams. But because it was very weedy it demanded special skills and tactics.

Owner Bill Lawrence "looked like an old cowboy," Parkening

said. Lawrence was a highly skilled fly fisher but also sometimes a hard, gruff man.

Parkening related a losing battle with a huge trout he once hooked and Lawrence's disparaging comment after the fish broke off : "That's no way to fight a big trout."

Parkening had followed the ranch rule to stay out of the water when fishing but he let the fish get too far away, so it made a right turn in the weeds and broke the small diameter leader. He then learned from Lawrence that "I had to stay close to a very large fish," and sometimes that meant jumping in the water to follow it.

In the spring creek most of the water was overgrown with watercress and other aquatic vegetation, with only a narrow open lane down the middle. Lawrence was a master dry fly technician, casting more than a twenty-foot leader and piling it up in the open water so the fly did not drag during the drift and Parkening learned to emulate him, honing skills that would serve him well the rest of his angling life. One useful technique was how to extract and land a fish that got into heavy weeds. He compared it to a minor first-aid procedure: "You pull out a splinter just like it went in."

All fly fishers are touched and changed by their own special waters and Hot Creek remains fresh and true in Parkening's memory. During his early life it was, he wrote in his book, "a spot that I loved more than any other place in the world."

Parkening's extraordinary natural musical talent and ueber-dedicated self discipline – reinforced, he said, by his father -- propelled him to recognition and fame in his mid-teens. His phenomenal playing progress in turn gave him access to the best teachers, from Celedonio and Pepe Romero to, eventually, Andrés Segovia, the legendary classical guitarist widely acknowledged during his lifetime as the greatest guitarist in the world.

Asked if fly fishing provided a respite from the structure and stress of his profession, or a continuation of the drive for perfection that marked his musical success, Parkening responded, "It's both." Wading a trout stream or drifting over a tarpon flat provides a refuge from the hurly-burly world of practice, travel, recording, and performing. But he emphasized that the laser focus and dedication required in his professional life have also served him well in his fly fishing.

In 1964, at age sixteen, Parkening attended a master class by Segovia, who told him he had "the potential for a wonderful career." He had come to believe Segovia's assertion that "the beauty of the guitar resides in its soft and persuasive voice, and its poetry cannot be equaled by any other instrument."

At age nineteen Parkening signed a six-album deal with Capitol Records and a year later embarked on a grueling concert schedule of sometimes ninety performances a year. Showing astonishing stamina, he performed in concerts, special appearances, and recording sessions for a decade with little rest or respite. Fame, fortune, and worldwide accolades became the hallmarks of his exceptional talent and dedication. Still, the stress of his profession's extraordinary physical and emotional demands prompted him to come up with a plan he clung to – to retire at thirty and fly fish for the rest of his life. He achieved his goal in 1977, buying a ranch with a beautiful spring type creek near Bozeman Montana, and ending all recording and touring.

He had made his choice, he said, because, "The most fun I've ever had in my life is fly fishing." And he made his fantasy life come true. He fly fished nearly every day in the warm months and spent the winters in Southern California. But within a couple of years a feeling of overwhelming emptiness and meaninglessness drove him to question his lifelong dream.

"I began to ask myself, 'If you have everything you ever wanted, but still there's that emptiness, what's left?' " he later wrote in his autobiography. The answer came through much soul-searching, which brought him to a religious epiphany: He became a Christian "to honor and glorify my Lord and Savior Jesus Christ."

Because he was raised as a Christian and baptized in early boyhood, Parkening always considered himself a Christian. But during his time of self reflection he came to the realization that most of his life had been spent pursuing his own needs, goals, and desires. A true Christian, he told himself, would devote his efforts to God's ends in the spirit of the Bible verse 1 Corinthians 10:31: "Whatsoever ye do, do all to the glory of God."

His spiritual transformation was prompted partly by attending services at Grace Community Church, pastored by John MacArthur, in Sun Valley, California, during his existential crisis. It was this California/Montana religious awakening that launched his second musical career and made him determined to dedicate his life – music, family, personal pursuits -- to God. When he made his choice he did not look back.

"When I became a Christian . . . I decided to sell this beautiful ranch," Parkening said of his onetime Montana dream property. He donated most of the money from the sale to Christian charities.

In *Grace Like a River* he explained in detail, "Buying a Montana ranch and trout stream had been my life's goal, and I had lived and breathed and played the guitar around the world in order to acquire my 'heaven on earth.' Now the fishing ranch became to me a symbol of my having something material more important than God."

After becoming a Christian, Parkening was determined to devote his future musical career to his faith, and cited Johann Sebastian Bach's pronouncement that, "The aim and final reason of all music should be none else but the glory of God." Through renewed persistence and determination, and despite the deep skepticism of friends and former associates, he re-established himself as a world-class classical guitarist, prompting *The Washington Post* to cite his stature as "the leading guitar virtuoso of our day, combining profound musical insight with complete technical mastery of his instrument."

After giving up his Montana ranch a fishing membership opened up at a ranch that had what he called "the best trout fishing I have ever known." At the time this chapter was written he had begun initiating his eight year old son, Luke, into the joys and mysteries of fly fishing. He was happily surprised that sometimes the student out-fished the teacher.

Dry fly trout fishing was Parkening's first love and it still enthralls him. But despite his everlasting love for trout, he has also pursued other, very different, quarry. He has no "favorite" kind of fly fishing and enjoys it whenever and wherever he can. However, he said, "There is no question that the most exciting fly fishing in the world is fly fishing for tarpon." The combination of huge, powerful fish that run, leap, and thrash as if possessed is special. "It's like being hooked to a freight train," he said.

The first time he fished for tarpon he was in Islamorada in the Florida Keys and on one-day notice called guide after guide trying to book a trip. Because it was high season all were booked, until he finally called Hank Brown, one of the Keys' top guides. Brown agreed to postpone a scheduled service on his motor because he thought the next day would be "perfect for tarpon fishing."

"We went to Nine-Mile Bank," Parkening said, and soon found the big fish. Parkening, cast to a dark spot in the water that Brown told him was actually a pod of tarpon and on his first cast hooked up a big silver king.

"We landed that fish and Hank Brown calls his wife," Parkening said. At that time there were no cell phones so Brown used his marine band radio. He had to tell her about his client, who had caught a trophy tarpon on the very first cast he made in his life. That day Parkening went on to hook seventeen fish and boat nine, an almost unheard-of accomplishment for a first-time tarpon angler.

Parkening returned to tarpon fishing in succeeding years, one year winning what was then the world's most prestigious tournament, the Florida Keys' International Gold Cup Tarpon Tournament, by boating a one hundred and thirty-seven pound fish.

At that time the tournament rules required competitors to bring in their catches for weighing. Despite the fish's size, Parkening's potential triumph was jeopardized when neither he nor his guide were able to gaff the tarpon at boatside. But in a show of fierce determination possessed only by the most driven anglers, Parkening leapt into the water and captured the tarpon by shoving his fist and arm into the fish's gill and out through its mouth. For his efforts he returned to the dock with his forearm torn and bloodied by the fish's gill rakers.

After becoming a Christian, Parkening came to view fly fishing from a different perspective. Gone was his earlier, self-centered approach, with its emphasis on personal gratification and fulfillment. Now, through fly fishing, "I can thank God for His incredible, awesome creation," he said.

Parkening retired from performing a few months before we spoke. Now, one of his main focuses is imparting his musical knowledge and skills to students in the master class he teaches at Pepperdine University in Malibu, California. Because Pepperdine is a Christian institution, he can also freely express his beliefs in the classroom. From his perspective at the pinnacle of his profession, he looks forward to many more years of personal ministry and sharing the ineffable mysteries of the classical guitar. And to wading waters both familiar and new.

The longing for one special, faraway adventure is innate to the sport's mystique and Parkening's was more specific than most. He had, he said, heard tales of Patagonia's huge sea-run browns, the flats bonanza of Christmas Island, and other exotic destinations. But his infatuation with dry fly trout fishing made his choice almost inevitable. "I have heard that on the South Island of New Zealand you can sight fish for ten-pound brown trout. So that would be my dream trip," he said.

Partially explaining the multifaceted significance of his book's title, Parkening said that, "Grace means God freely giving you something you don't deserve . . . . And fly fishing is part of God's grace that he has bestowed on me." Speaking with him and reading *Grace Like a River* prompts one to consider other meanings: the grace of a well-made cast; the riffled ebb and surge of a mountain stream; a trout, quick and numinous, slipping away into the flow. The grace of sweet, sacred music played by a master. And the grace of a life well lived by an extraordinary man.

Chapter 9
Bill Ford:
Industrialist, Iconoclast, Environmentalist

Though born a scion of one of America's foremost families, William Clay Ford, Jr. (he prefers "Bill"), executive chairman of Ford Motor Company, has never been content to ride to success on the coattails of his illustrious heritage. Born in 1957, he showed his self reliance early, including in his fiercely competitive boyhood pursuit of team sports (especially ice hockey and rugby), then later through his academic accomplishments at Princeton (BA) and the Massachusetts Institute of Technology (SM).

Ford Motor Company

Working his way up the corporate ladder at Ford Motor over more than two decades, Bill Ford championed innovative and sometimes iconoclastic approaches to business methods and philosophy, including his signature issue: transforming the automobile industry's environmental stance. His commitment to producing cleaner, more fuel efficient cars helped bring about a sea change in the industry's attitude from opposition and skepticism to acceptance of the idea that the greening of the Big Three is compatible with the goals of robust production and profits.

Bill Ford's tireless efforts to reduce greenhouse gases in the ongoing fight for the future of the earth are widely known. Less well known is just how significant a role fly fishing has played in shaping his environmental ethos and driving his efforts. Talking with him the point came across very forcefully.

"There's no question that my . . . environmental bent came from my love of the outdoors, which came from my love of fly fishing," he said." It's a pretty direct correlation, frankly. As I spent more and more time in the outdoors as a young man, the more I grew to love the outdoors. I remember even as a very young man going to places that had once been pristine and all of a sudden had been ruined either through pollution or development. I remember thinking . . . how sad that was. That clearly shaped my early thinking toward environmentalism and the need to be stewards of the environment."

Like so many highly successful people who are also passionate fly fishers, Ford has fished over a good portion of the world for a wide variety of species: brown trout in England's legendary chalk streams, peacock bass in the steamy Amazon, bonefish in the Keys, huge salmon and trout in Argentina and Alaska. But despite his travels to exotic locales, his home waters still exert the strongest pull.

"I love every kind of fly fishing," Ford said, "and I'll never turn down an opportunity to go to do anything. But if I had one day to spend it would be a small river in northern Michigan (the Lower

Peninsula) dry fly fishing." His love affair with the region of thick forests and richly prolific trout streams, which began when he was five, was nurtured by a special mentor.

"My parents belonged to a fishing club in northern Michigan which had been around since the turn of the last century," Ford remembered. The club was Fontinalis -- from Salvelinus fontinalis, the Latin designation for brook trout, the region's signature salmonid species – on the banks of the Sturgeon River.

"My mother took me up when I was around that age," he said, "and there was a caretaker there who took me into the woods – I was fascinated, not just by the fishing, which I learned to love, but also just by the stories he could tell me about the woods, the plants, the animals. And then, when we got actually to the fishing, about the fish, what they ate, why the trout lie, where they lie, their feeding patterns."

The mentor's name was Walter Babcock. In sharing his breadth of knowledge about the outdoors and love of all things wild, Babcock helped shape Ford's outlook and life goals, at the same time imparting a near-obsessive love of fly fishing that has never diminished. From their times spent together in the woods and on the water grew a lifelong friendship.

Ford's infatuation with the sport continued to grow in the years following his first exposure. "Every year for my birthday I would ask my parents for my birthday present to give me another trip back up there," he said. "And . . . as soon as I got my driver's license at age sixteen I threw all my gear in the back of my car and drove up to northern Michigan whenever I could."

As befits his favorite region, Ford's most beloved quarry is brook trout. But he qualified his preference with one telling phrase: "during the day." For in his late preteen years he contracted another strain of the fly fishing bug – also introduced to him by Babcock -- that remains highly virulent: night fishing for browns.

"What we get in Michigan which is interesting, most people don't know," he explained, "is we have a year-round resident brown population and they are fine and they grow up to be probably, eighteen, nineteen inches for the largest ones. But what we also have, which are why we do the night fishing, are the lake run browns that come out of the Great Lakes."

The lake fish begin moving into the streams in early summer in preparation for the fall spawn. In late summer, he related, "they're up there in big numbers but you'll never see them during the day. They sit underneath the undercut banks and they don't come out. And they get up to twelve, thirteen, fourteen pounds. The largest I've ever landed is nine."

It is a challenging, sometimes maddening, kind of fishing. "You lose many more than you land," Ford said, "because there are all these overgrown branches and trees and they wrap you around and they're gone. But to have them on for just a few minutes is still a blast."

Ford's best fishing buddy is his lifelong friend Steven Phinny, who at the time this chapter was written was also his partner in the Scott rod company. The two purchased Scott in 1987 and "have fished all over together." One of the most important reasons for their compatibility and ongoing partnership on the water, Ford said, is their similar approach to the sport.

"You know, it's interesting, I'm a very competitive person," Ford explained, "and so is he. But the one thing we're not remotely competitive about is fly fishing." The idea of keeping score like some anglers – biggest fish, most fish, etc. -- is anathema to them both.

Fishing with someone who is very competitive is "no fun at all" Ford said. "I guess I'm so happy just to be out there that I don't really much care. It's great if I'm having a good day but if I'm not and he is then that's great too."

The allure of far-flung angling destinations beckons many fly fishers; there are is always one more "last best place," another fish that reputedly outfights or out-dazzles all others. But Ford's response to the question whether there is a dream trip he has not made was emphatic: "No. Because there are plenty of places I would be thrilled to go. But I kind of feel like I'm just happy when I can get to any river. . . . There are a lot of things I haven't done that I'd love to do. I think it would be fun to fish for the big brook trout in Labrador, I've never done that. I've never caught an Atlantic salmon, I'd like to do that. I guess there's a lot I've never done, but on the other hand I've also done a lot. To me, I'd be just as happy to throw my stuff in the car and go up to northern Michigan as to take some exotic trip."

When we talked, Ford's fly fishing was more and more a family affair. He and his wife, Lisa Vanderzee, have four children, and at the time all were adults or fast approaching adulthood. All had fly fished and the two younger ones Will and Nick, seemed to Ford to be as hooked as their dad.

He related in earlier years sometimes going fly fishing and not even taking a rod. Instead, he would "just put my waders on and wade next to them, particularly my younger son (Nick). . . . Or take one rod between the two of us. The thrill for him, Ford said, was "to watch him tie a fly on, make the cast and then hook the fish. It was a sea change from their earliest times together on the water when Ford, much as many fathers have done, would make a cast and let Nick fight the fish. He viewed his role as more guide than fellow fly fisher.

Ford believed, he said, that fly fishing has different lessons to teach but downplayed his expertise and judgment, unwilling to make grandiose pronouncements about other people's feelings and ideas. "Well, I'm probably not the greatest philosopher in the world," he said. "I think probably because it teaches everybody something different. Some people it probably teaches patience, for others it may teach them appreciation of the outdoors, others it might teach them just to slow a little in their lives. But for me it (the most important lesson) really was a lifelong love of the natural world, which translated in my professional life into a very strong environmental ethic."

When this chapter was written, examples of how Bill Ford had converted his ecological ethos into concrete results could be seen throughout Ford Motor Company's production policies and vehicle lineup. And, in an encouraging sign that other manufacturers have also climbed aboard the environmental bandwagon, throughout other car companies' lineups as well.

In the company's 2011/2012 annual Sustainability Report Bill Ford enumerated some of the company's progress toward protecting the environment. "The . . . approach is . . . behind the rapid transformation of our vehicle fleet into a leader in fuel economy and other attributes our customers value," Ford wrote. "And it's helping keep us on track to meet our goal to reduce carbon dioxide (CO_2) emissions from our vehicles in every region in order to address the climate change issue. For example, through the use of our EcoBoost® turbocharged, direct-injection gas engines and other features spelled out in our Sustainable Technologies and Alternative Fuels plan, we have improved the fuel economy of our U.S. vehicles by nearly 17 percent since 2006." Ford also pointed out that "nearly one-third of Ford's vehicle lines in the U.S. will feature a model with 40 mpg or more in 2012 – a claim no other full-line automaker can match."

But just as salient as the facts that fly fishing informed his world view and underpinned his principles was the sport's other role in Ford's life – a joyful diversion. And he left no room for doubt where it ranked among his free-time pastimes: "Right at the top. There's nothing I'd rather do. My other great passion is I play ice hockey. But if I only had one activity I could do and only a day or so to do it I would clearly pick fly fishing."

Ford said that, however far and wide he fished, he would return again and again to his beloved northern Michigan. "It's what I grew up with and I know those waters so well and when I get out West and I fish the big waters I don't know how to read them very well. . . . If I have somebody with me, a guide or something, it's helpful but then I feel like why do I need a guide? I've been fishing my whole life. When I fish small streams I feel very at home, I know exactly what I'm looking at, I feel like I can do that as well as anyone, and I really enjoy it."

Ford, who worked for several years overseas during his younger years, was not enamored of the sport's strictures there. "It's weird," he said. "I used to live in England and I'd get on some of those beats. Interesting, but I thought, I mean, it was so stylized and you couldn't cast until you saw a rise. To me it's all interesting but it wasn't my favorite way to fish."

Ford's less than fond recollection of his British experiences provided a sharp contrast to wistful reminiscences about his formative fly fishing years with Babcock at Fontinalis, near the tiny little town of Vanderbilt, Michigan. "He only passed away a few years ago well into his 90s," Ford remembered. "And what was really amazing about him was that even at the very end of his life he would go night fishing by himself. He'd lie to his wife and say he was going with friends. He'd disappear into the cedar swamps, and there are lots of beaver holes and he could have broken a leg very easily out there."

"I asked him, you know, Walter I'm worried about going by yourself. Or he'd lie to her and tell her I was up for the weekend even when I wasn't, and we were going together, which we often did when I was up. I said, you know, I'm really worried about you and he said, 'So what's the worst that could happen? I die by the river and that's not a bad way to go.' "

It is a declaration that it would not be hard to imagine Ford making himself.

Chapter 10
Mary Alice Monroe:
Classy Writer, Classic Conservationist

For New York Times bestselling author Mary Alice Monroe, nature and humanity are inextricably linked. In her work and in her world view she draws no sharp dividing lines among forests, mountains, rivers, oceans, wild creatures, people, and the complex circle of existence. All are part of a continuum that also encompasses the vicissitudes of the human experience -- good, bad, and indifferent -- including those most human of strengths and frailties: faith, hope, sorrow, suffering, and the mystery of imagination.

Mary Alice Monroe

But despite the deep spirituality of her outlook -- evocative of Transcendentalism -- Monroe is no New-Age dreamer. She is a highly disciplined and prolific writer, an accomplished academic and multilingual internationalist, ardent conservationist, wife, mother, and grandmother, and the author of one of the most affecting fly fishing novels of recent years: *Time is a River*. Set mostly in the mountains and trout streams of North Carolina, this book is a lovely, belletristic paean to the sport, mostly seen through the eyes of a woman who is recovering from breast cancer. It is also a story of love, loss and redemption sparked by the recovery of a region's hidden (fictional) past.

At the time this chapter was written, Monroe had recently finished her fourteenth book, *The Butterfly's Daughter,* partly a treatise on the saga of the monarch butterfly, which migrates often more than a thousand miles to over-winter in Mexico, returning north in the spring to reproduce.

Monroe's work is distinctive for the nuanced hues and finely textured brush strokes of her character portraits – her main protagonists are usually women – as well as for her dramatic plots interwoven with nature themes: i.e. fly fishing, sea turtles, birds of prey. To abuse a lame pun, nature themes come naturally to her from her earliest childhood.

"When I was very young it (nature) was more fanciful," she said. "I had an incredible imagination and I would think of fairies and elves and hunt for them in the woods. As I got older my father would take us for walks in the woods and would point out the names of trees. . . . And my family . . . has a farm in Vermont and would spend their summers there. And there would always be a list of what birds were sighted and they were always very concerned about conservation. . . . And I think with my own children I have tried to incorporate both the fanciful – they all looked for fairies when they were young – and they also know the names of the trees and the birds and the butterflies."

Growing up in Evanston, Illinois, Monroe attended Northwestern University but did not finish college in her first stint. "I married young and moved with my husband to New Jersey and then from New Jersey to Washington, D.C.," she said. In those early years of married life the young couple led eventful lives, including an intriguing summer spent in Japan that piqued her interest in the culture.

"When I returned I knew that I wanted to study Japanese," she said. "I don't know, I must have been Japanese in another life. I came home and I began studying Japanese in earnest. I changed my major in college, went back to school and I studied for seven years and I ended up getting a master's degree in Japanese and teaching. And I still speak Japanese, it's still a passion of mine."

When she started at Northwestern after high school, Monroe's ambition had been to be a writer. But events – marriage, her Japanese studies, teaching, becoming a young mother, the family's frequent moves – intervened, providing ready-made excuses not to write. Then, in one of the more quirky writer's beginnings, free time was forced upon her.

"When I was pregnant with my third child I was confined to bed," she said. "It's kind of a humbling experience because I was in bed for four months and I couldn't even sit up. . . . And my husband, who's a psychiatrist, said to me, 'You know Mary' – I was feeling very sorry for myself – 'Mary Alice you have a choice. You can either sit here and watch TV and kind of wallow your time or you can write a book. You've always wanted to write a book for as long as I've known you.' "

"I realized that I might not have that gift of time again so that's exactly what I kept thinking. So I wrote my first novel, sort of started it in bed, and I moved on to finish it after the baby was born. You know, there's a saying that seems to follow me but it really is true, that I gave birth to a baby and a book," she said, laughing. But although she made light of it, Monroe considered it an epiphany.

"Seeing the glass half full rather than half empty -- is the lesson that I learned," she said. "Sometimes what looks like the worst thing in the world that could happen to you, if you look at it with an open mind you realize it can be an opportunity. . . . Life is a series of ups and downs and it's all about how you address them, how you face them."

A move to the South Carolina Low Country in 1999 was a seminal event for both Monroe's family and for her development as a writer. "We had been coming here for ten years prior. So we knew we wanted to come here eventually. . . . It opened up all kinds of possibilities as a writer. It was a combination of timing, the right time and the right place," she said. "Because I was at an age when my children were older and I jumped into my mission. I put all the things that I had learned throughout all my life about nature and conservation. And when I came to this area where I could see so clearly how quickly things could change in the landscape then I knew I had a mission. And it was really a decision on my part when I prepared to write novels that would encourage an awareness of what we have and what we could lose. . . . All my novels are character driven, about life, especially a woman's life. But when I moved to South Carolina my career markedly changed. And that was when I made the decision to set my books against some aspect of nature that needed to have a heightened awareness. It started with the sea turtles."

Despite discouraging words from editors ("who wants to read about turtles?"), she wrote *The Beach House* which partly chronicled the plight of sea turtles. "So I handed it in," she said, "and I knew I'd done something different, and it was my first New York Times hit. And I think it was a response to the reader to this niche that I'd created. . . . It was like everything in my life had crystallized."

Monroe had fished off and on throughout her life but her

induction into fly fishing came in 2005 when she read an article in the Charleston Post and Courier about women fly fishers and hooked up with a group called The Damsel Fly Fishers. Soon afterward she went to a local fly shop to "outfit" herself. Looking back, she spoke about it sheepishly.

"I should never have outfitted myself until I had my preferences known," she said, chuckling. "You know that and now I know that but at the time I didn't, and I bought a lot of stuff. And I went up with a group of five women, six including myself, and we went up to see Starr Nolan." Nolan is a world renowned fly angler and guide who specializes in western North Carolina and also heads Casting for Recovery (the breast cancer therapy outings) in the Carolinas and Georgia.

"She owns her own fly fishing tour company called Brookside Guides," Monroe continued. "And she was their friend and mentor. She always took this group out on trips. I was very excited and I went up to the Davidson."

"We went up there, it was a beautiful day, we went up with a group, you know. But when we got to the river and we walked down the slope . . . all the women began to fan out. And I stayed with Starr. I looked down over the water and I saw how all the women were slowly getting acclimated to the area," she recalled. "It was a beautiful spring morning, there was that mist that comes up early in the morning from the water, and there were butterflies everywhere, this was in North Carolina, and you almost had to bat them away. It was mystical it was so beautiful. And these women, I noticed them putting on their gear, and looking at the water, and picking up the rocks and really becoming aware of the place. And one by one they went into their own individual four-count rhythm. I didn't know at that point exactly what I was observing. But I knew intuitively that these were women who were very much in the know. They were in their own world, they were connected to that river. And it was so beautiful, I'll never forget that."

"Then Starr began to teach me," she said, "but I already knew this was a sport for me. And honestly I think the reason I wrote *Time is a River* the way I did is as I grew better over the next couple of years and I learned different kinds of techniques, I think what I loved about Mia (the book's main character and breast cancer survivor) was how clumsy she was. It was how I was for so long. You know, you don't just pick up a fly rod and start casting beautifully across the water. You catch the trees, you catch the rocks, you catch your pants. You don't know one fly from the other. But when you catch that fish and you bring it in and you hold that trout in your hand and you release it back into the water there's a bond that's created, you feel that visceral connection to that fish and the world around you that is so healing that I knew that's what I had to write about; I knew it. So for years I researched it before I felt ready to write that book."

"I really wanted to write a book about fly fishing. . . . I just kind of clicked, you know. . . . rivers, trout, the mountains. . . . I can't explain what it is when I know I'm onto something and it's very intuitive."

Not surprisingly, Monroe's favorite kind of fly fishing is for trout in mountain streams. "I really prefer it," she said. "I'm not all that experienced. I haven't fished many different rivers. I tend to go to North Carolina a lot and I've done some bone fishing in the Bahamas. So that's pretty much my experience."

But like most fly fishers she dreams of broadening her angling horizons. "I know that I do want to get into the rough waters," she said. "My girlfriends have houses in Montana. And I know that's completely another type. And Alaska's a dream. The Damsel Fly Fishers go almost every year to Alaska. And I just have such a tough time managing my career with the pace of publishing that I have that it's all I can do to just get up to North Carolina and do my little fly fishing. And that I need for my mental health. I'm not trying to learn something new as much as just to escape."

Heading the list of her favorite spots is her natal river, the Davidson. "I think it's because I know it so well," she said. "Also, there's a little place up in Nashville. It's a small lake and it's connected to a little retreat area. And it's very quiet and very still. And I sometimes go there because of the little cabin that someone lets me have. And it's private, privately owned. But I can just go and kind of escape there. It's not very powerful. It's more just knowing where the fish are and testing out different flies; and practicing my rusty casting. . . . It's really where I can go just to escape."

Monroe did not hesitate to list fly fishing as "right at the top" of her favorite free time activities, and like many busy professionals she vowed to make more time for it. "I am going to try to get out more, out to different rivers more," she said. "I have friends and family in the Chattanooga area and Tennessee has great fishing. It's more about time. Just the escape time, to take vacation."

As one would expect from a world-class writer, she is very articulate about her reasons for loving fly fishing. "To cut everything off and to go into nature, to go to the river, and stand in the water, that's what fly fishing's about," she said. "It isn't about going out and catching that fish, it's about being connected to the fish, to understanding the water, and paying attention to the small details. And that connection to nature as a whole, I think, is calming. That connection to something bigger than ourselves puts our ego into correct perspective. It makes you feel both smaller and part of something much bigger than yourself. I think fly fishing more than anything else gives you that exercise in connection."

Monroe recalled with self-deprecating humor the comedy of errors that occurred when she met up with a USA Today reporter after the publication of *Time is a River* to take him fly fishing. Fishing the rain-swollen -- and ironically named -- Dry Creek in Virginia, she and her friend Starr Nolan demonstrated how to fish in raging, muddy, windy conditions.

Now imagine this," she said. "This is the film crew, the big re-porter, Craig Wilson from USA Today, Starr, and me, we climbed down this slope, covered now with mud. And you know what it's like when you cast into the wind. And on my bad side, with my left arm, because it was the only spot we could even get close to the wa-ter, where we would not be washed away. There were tree boughs everywhere. I think I caught every leaf in the area, but we certainly did not catch any fish. And it was a very amusing review, a very nice article actually, he was very kind. And in the end – just to show you how things work out – both Craig and I laughed. And I said, You know, Craig, I'm glad it turned out this way because I want the readers to know, and all the people who think fly fishing's only for the experts, that it's okay not to catch a fish."

Her favorite species is the shy native char of her home waters: brook trout. "I think they're so unassuming," she said. "They're much more of a challenge to catch."

Among her fly fishing goals for the future one takes precedence. "Just to always plug Casting for Recovery," she said. It's such a wonderful organization. And when I was working with the women with cancer, the survivors who faced death so much, it truly was transforming to see their faces light up. . . . And whether or not they ever fish again – a large number of them continue fishing – it's just reminding them what life is all about."

"Whether you're a survivor of cancer, or a survivor of any of the many traumas we all go through. That is the beauty of connection, especially fly fishing, that when you see the fish and you see the connection, then you release that life back into the wilderness, that you are reminded that life goes on, that you are part of that river. And I think that was the key to the book, and what they learn in Casting for Recovery and how most people feel if they really under-stand the art of fly fishing."

Chapter 11
Jack Nicklaus:
An Athlete's Spirit

Despite a plethora of short- and long-term challengers over more than four decades, there is little doubt that Jack Nicklaus is the greatest golfer of all time. His record of eighteen major tournaments and seventy-one Professional Golf Association tour wins stands alone. When this chapter was written, Nicklaus' nearest rival, Tiger Woods (fourteen major wins), once highly touted to outdo "The Golden Bear," seemed destined to fall short as his own career wound down.

The Nicklaus Companies

Nicklaus, whose PGA years lasted from 1961 to 1986, transformed the game into a mega-spectator sport, a television phenomenon and a sponsor juggernaut. These days he remains passionate about all aspects of his sport/profession, from designing courses to playing in exhibition tournaments. But there is another sporting activity he avidly pursues and has made it a point to master: fly fishing.

Nicklaus' young boyhood and teen years in Upper Arlington (near Columbus), Ohio, provided early evidence of his natural athleticism. In addition to golf, he played football, baseball and tennis, and competed in track and field. During his senior year in high school he was named an All-Ohio selection in basketball, which he played as a guard.

But though he did well at all competitive sports, he excelled from the beginning at golf. The first time he played, at ten, he shot a fifty-one for nine holes at Scioto Country Club, a local venue. At twelve he won his first of five Ohio Junior Championships. At fourteen he won the Tri-State (Ohio, Indiana, Kentucky) High School Championship.

After high school, at Ohio State, Nicklaus quickly began building his legend, winning two U.S. Amateur titles and the 1961 NCAA Championship. At the 1960 U.S. Open, playing as an amateur, he finished second to Arnold Palmer. From 1959 to 1961 Golf Digest magazine named him the world's best amateur golfer.

Nicklaus turned pro in late 1961, cutting short his studies at Ohio State a few courses short of a degree. Eleven years later the school awarded him an honorary doctorate.

His first PGA victory came with an explosion of publicity and instant nationwide fame when he topped Palmer at the 1962 Open. The win put him on the cover of Time magazine and began a career trajectory that took him to sports legend status in a few years.

A year later he won both the Masters and the PGA Championship. Eventually he became the first triple Grand-Slam winner (in 1978), and during his career won four U.S. Opens, Five PGA Championships, and six Masters. The last Masters he won in 1986 at forty-six years old, putting the lie to one malicious golf writer's pronouncement that he was "washed up."

Since getting his last PGA win and closing out his full-time twenty-five year PGA career in 1986, Nicklaus has written books, designed courses, created video games, and played on the Champions Tour (for over-fifty pros). He also played at the 1998 Masters, earning accolades for his sixth-place finish at the age of fifty-eight. He has also fly fished; a lot.

Growing up, Nicklaus led a typical Midwestern boy's life in which the outdoors – especially hunting and fishing – played its customary part. As a pre-teen and teenager his fishing gear of choice was spinning or bait casting tackle. Though he was in the process of becoming a golf prodigy, Nicklaus recalls those years as also punctuated by "occasional spin or bait casting, but I was never really much of a fisherman." It was during his college years at Ohio State – when he surged into the national limelight as a golfer -- that he also first started fly fishing. It was love at first cast, he remembers, because "it was an art and it was a challenge and I thought it was probably the most sporting way to catch a fish."

As for many of us, some of the details of Nicklaus' early fly fishing forays have faded from memory over the intervening decades, but the remembrance of how naturally the sport came to him remains vivid.

"I'm not sure how I learned," he said. "It came fairly easy to me. When you're a kid and you're a good athlete, most everything came easy. I never really thought much about learning."

In the years since his natal angling experiences, fly fishing has become – after golf – Nicklaus' other major life pursuit. And he has the flying miles and stream and flats time to prove it. In January 2010 he celebrated his seventieth birthday in the middle of the Pacific prowling the shallows for bonefish on Christmas Island. He has fished from Montana to New Zealand, Key West to Cancun, and many waters in between.

Nicklaus spoke somewhat dismissively of his early efforts as "just trout fishing." He made it clear, however, that he was not denigrating the salmonids -- still some of his most prized quarry -- but simply downplaying his rudimentary skills.

From the basic small-stream, ten o'clock-two o'clock cast, Nicklaus progressed to more advanced techniques with the help of his father, Charlie, and two luminaries of twentieth century angling: Henry Shakespeare, owner of the Shakespeare Rod Company, and company vice president Ben Hardesty, a seven-time U.S. casting champion.

"Ben taught me to double haul," Nicklaus recalls. "And once I learned to double haul, then fly fishing became a lot more fun, a lot easier, conditions didn't bother you as much. And then it was a matter of learning and growing from there." Growing included expanding his angling horizons to salt water.

These days his preferences are eclectic. "I enjoy all the freshwater fishing. I love to fish for salmon, I love to fish for trout, but I still think the challenge of the bonefish or permit on a fly is probably what I enjoy more," he said. "I like tarpon fishing but . . . I actually prefer the smaller tarpon over the larger tarpon because it's kind of more action. But I like all of them. But if I had a day of fishing I had to go do, I'd probably go bonefishing."

Even for a world-class athlete, there are some sporting goals that are harder to reach than others. At the time of our interview Nicklaus had a photo of a permit he caught "ten or twelve years ago" hanging on the wall in his office. "I've only caught two on a fly. Both in the Marquesas," he said. He ruefully recounted a near-miss trip to Royal Island, Bahamas. "What was it, a month or two I was over there?" he rhetorically asked himself. "I had two of them bury the fly and I missed them both," he continued, his words inflected with harsh self-criticism. "Two of them within an hour."

When it comes to favorite fishing spots, Nicklaus favored two dissimilar but famously familiar destinations. "Probably the Bahamas and New Zealand," he said. "Because I like bone fishing, but I love the trip to New Zealand."

However, his preferences are not set in stone. "I keep pursuing dream trips I haven't made," he said. . . . As I understand it, there's some really good bonefishing in the South Pacific I'm exploring.

I'm trying to figure out where and how that is. New Caledonia. I understand."

In his attitude and approach toward fly fishing, the champion athlete's fiercely competitive spirit shone through. There is nothing laid-back or (to use the irritatingly ubiquitous cliché) "Zen-like" about it.

"I don't use it for relaxation," he asserted. "I use it because I want to do it. Does it relax me? Yes. But I use it because I like the competition, I use it because it's fun." On average, he fly fishes about thirty days a year, or "three days a month, almost."

One result of his long association with the sport is a common one: a greater appreciation for the resource. "It's made me more of an environmentalist. Absolutely," he says. "I mean, years ago everybody killed their fish. I haven't killed a fish in twenty, twenty-five years. Other than a fish to eat, tuna or something like that. I catch and release everything now. I have for years."

Nicklaus' conservation ethos evinces itself in other ways. From 2006 to 2009 Nicklaus was a national spokesman for the Federation of Fly Fishers, the fly fishing fraternity/sorority cum clean water and conservation advocacy group founded in the early 1960s by some of the giants of the sport, including Lee Wulff, Ted Trueblood, Ed Zern, Pete Hidy, Polly Rosborough, et al.

Nicklaus' efforts on behalf of the FFF included fund raising and enhancing the profile of the organization and its causes, especially its environmental and educational campaigns.

R.P. "Pete" Van Gytenbeek, former head of both Trout Unlimited and the Federation of Fly Fishers, was the one who persuaded Nicklaus to lend his fame and influence to the FFF. Van Gytenbeek recalled hearing an account from a mutual friend about a trip Nicklaus made to Tierra del Fuego to fish for the region's giant sea-run browns.

"The weather was apparently abominable," Van Gytenbeek says.

"He (the friend) said that Nicklaus was in the adjoining club. They were kind of on the same water on opposite sides of the stream just talking back and forth as best they could in the wind and the rain, and he just fished *all* day. There was no way this guy was going to quit. He said, 'I went in and had lunch, came back out and Nicklaus was still whaling away and had caught one while I was gone.' "

"He's just a dead serious fisherman and a beautiful caster under horrible conditions," Van Gytenbeek said.

There are many reasons that fly fishing heads the list of Nicklaus' favorite free-time pursuits. One is the natural segue from the fiercely competitive world of professional sports. Self abnegation, focus and dedication, come naturally to sports heroes. They embrace challenges and expect no quarter from opponents. These traits also serve fly fishers well. The "competition" is with the fish and, more importantly, themselves. Trying to discover what a trout is rising to or what a bonefish is tailing for, then planning the stalk and cast, is like figuring out how to hit a golf ball in a tough lie or how a putt will track toward the hole.

For Jack Nicklaus, still undisputed all-time best golfer, fly fishing's biggest appeal is "definitely discipline. It's also fair chase. And it doesn't always work. Sometimes the fish don't want that fly."

And though he has fished far and wide with different angling friends, Nicklaus' favorite companions are the closest to home: "My wife, my family."

Chapter 12
Sandra Day O'Connor: Ground-Breaking Jurist, Lifelong Outdoorswoman

As a girl growing up in the Southwest, Sandra Day O'Connor was not exactly blessed with circumstances conducive to becoming an angler. In fact, O'Connor, a retired United States Supreme Court justice and the first woman to serve on the High Court, faced perhaps the most insurmountable challenge for any prospective fly fisher: lack of water.

United States Supreme Court

"I grew up on a very remote ranch in Arizona and New Mexico. And we saved every drop of water. We didn't have any fishing available," she said. Her childhood on the 155,000-acre Lazy-B was defined by horses, cattle, harsh climate, and mile after mile of arid countryside underlain by volcanic rock.

"The rainfall averages ten inches a year or less. . . . It was no country for sissies," O'Connor and her brother H. Alan Day, wrote in their joint autobiography: *Lazy B: Growing up on a Cattle Ranch in the American Southwest*. They wrote of days "so quiet you can hear a beetle scurrying across the ground;" and nights punctuated by the wailing calls of coyotes. Rain was "the most treasured event – prayed for hoped for, anticipated, savored, treasured, celebrated, and enjoyed."

Though it did not directly foster her later love of fly fishing, the ranch's arduous work, climate, and geography did instill in her a lifelong love of wide-open spaces and rigorous outdoor activities. It also helped make her physically fit and developed her lifelong love of athletic endeavors, especially tennis.

As a counterbalance to the isolation – the nearest school was twenty-two miles away – Sandra Day's parents, Harry A. and Ada Mae Wilkey Day, sent her to live with her maternal grandmother in El Paso, Texas, for all but one year of elementary and high school. At sixteen she headed off to Stanford University.

Before starting her studies at Stanford, where she received a BA in Economics and an LL.B, the only chances O'Connor got to wet a line took place during trips with her parents to the Sea of Cortez (also called the Gulf of California), between the Mexican mainland and Baja California. "And that was not fly fishing," O'Connor said. After her Magna Cum Laude graduation from Stanford in 1950, O'Connor told in her book, the Day family made a trip to Alaska, where they reveled in the lush, moist landscape and "caught a few fish." Soon after, she entered Stanford Law School.

In a sense, one of O'Connor's early adult life experiences was as harsh as the natural environment on the Day ranch. In 1952, after graduating third in her class from one of the country's top law schools, she ran into the concrete wall of the era's insidious sex discrimination. Every law firm she applied to refused to hire her as an attorney. In what amounted to a stark example of women's untenable situation in the career world, she received one offer to be a legal secretary. She finally took a position as an assistant county attorney in California.

Also in 1952, Sandra Day married fellow Stanford Law School alumnus – he had graduated one year ahead of her -- John Jay O'Connor and, after John's military service in Germany, they moved to the Phoenix area. When her three children were very young, O'Connor, worked part time as an attorney with her husband. But beginning in the early 1960s she began seriously pursuing a full-time career of public service and activism in Republican politics that came to include a term as assistant attorney general of Arizona, three terms in the state Senate, and, in 1979, an appointment to the state's Court of Appeals. In 1981 President Ronald Reagan broke nearly two centuries of shameful neglect with her appointment to the nation's top judicial body.

When discussing her life and fly fishing, O'Connor, showed the circumspection of many high-profile federal government officials about revealing details of travels and friendships, an unfortunate necessity in today's world of omnipresent security concerns.

A deep and abiding passion infused her account of how she came to the sport, "late in life." One of her first experiences came during a 1980 trip to New Zealand with her husband. She spoke of it with self-deprecating humor.

"I didn't know what I was doing," she said. "The fishing in New Zealand is hard, because the water is so clear. You fish at midnight on a dark night without a moon or they're gonna see you coming. But it was fun, and I did try. And in the intervening years I've had two or three opportunities to go to Alaska and of course that fishery. . . there is nothing to top it. I just love it. And I'm going to go again this summer.

Not long after her excursion Down Under, she continued her angling apprenticeship with "a very good friend here in Arizona, a wonderful fly fisherman, and we practiced how to fly fish a little bit and I went a couple of times with him."

But O'Connor's skill advancement and enthusiasm for the sport -- paralleling the astonishing trajectory of her career – truly began with President Ronald Reagan's 1981 appointment of her to the Supreme Court.

"When we moved back to Washington, D.C., I met a fellow who actually *taught* fly fishing (she could not recall his name). And I had him give me some lessons and we went out to some ponds. And it was fun and I started to learn. And then I was invited to go out to Montana, and I stayed at a place along Slough Creek in Yellowstone. And so I was able to fish Slough Creek. And that was so fabulous, I just adored it. And that got me hooked. More than the fish, it hooked me." She was hooked so completely that no other type of fishing held any interest for her.

Since her initial Montana foray, O'Connor had broadened her fly fishing horizons. One of her favorite destinations remained Alaska. "There is nothing to top it. I just love it," she said. "And I'm going to go again this summer."

"So that is wonderful, and then I have good friends who have a summer residence in Montana and I have managed to go up there about every year for a little fishing in different places in Montana. And I just have had wonderful experiences fly fishing. And there is a club in Pennsylvania called Blooming Grove and I've been very privileged to fish there a few times."

There have been other places, near and far: Yellowstone National Park, the Missouri "a time or two."

"I have fished in the Sun Valley area, too," she said. "That's kind of nice. I've even done that in the winter. Because I had fallen and I had a ski injury and I couldn't ski. So while my family was skiing I went out with a guide in the winter. And we caught a few fish in the river (the Big Wood) there in Sun Valley.

"I also made a trip one time to Mongolia, and that was pretty exciting," she continued. "They have taimen up there . . . and then they have another fish that's kind of like a trout. But that was fun, to fish in Mongolia." She made the trip with her husband. Though she did not elaborate, O'Connor had to cope with her husband's severe Alzheimer's disease for nearly two decades. John O'Connor died in a care facility in 2009.

O'Connor showed no hesitation in naming her favorite kind of fly fishing. "Trout fishing in a stream. I like to walk. I prefer that to a boat. I like to be in a stream, take my time, and do it that way." The Spokesman-Review newspaper in Spokane, Washington, in a 2005 feature about the justice, jumped at the chance to use the type of first-rate groaner pun so beloved by journalists, referring to O'Connor's preference as "her definitive decision on Row v. Wade."

Her favorite fly is a Parachute Adams, the all-purpose mayfly used to approximate so many hatches.

As for fly fishing having had any influence on her personal and professional life, O'Connor dismissed the notion with the no-nonsense bluntness of a dry-land rancher and strict constructionist jurist.

"No, of course not. But it's a good diversion. When you're fly fishing you have to be totally concentrating. You can't let your eyes stray for a second or you're gonna have a problem. And so you can't be thinking about some legal problem, you have to be thinking about the fish and your fly."

When she was at the Supreme Court she took her law clerks on fly fishing outings, sometimes along the Potomac, a very good smallmouth fishery.

She did acknowledge that, because of the focus required, fly fishing is "in a way" an escape valve. "It means you're not thinking about some other problem or you're gonna miss all the fish," she said.

When asked if the sport had anything to teach people, she hesitated, seemingly wary about imparting any highfalutin mysticism to the pastime.

"Well, I don't know. It's just a wonderful thing because it takes a certain amount of skill," she said. "You have to be engaged in a lot of moments. You're walking, you're trying to cast well, you're trying to put the fly where you want it. It requires a lot of effort and concentration. And it's in beautiful places. And I just get very excited when there's a fish on the line. I can't help myself, I think it's great. And I like to let 'em go, I don't keep them. I try to treat them gently and let them go. And I use barbless hooks and try to treat 'em right. And I think you can do that and not damage the fish."

But despite her skepticism about any deeper meaning, she made it clear that the sport had affected some of her own views, especially on conservation. "I care very much about keeping those streams in good shape and taking care of the fisheries, the habitat, of course," she said.

Like many fly fishers, O'Connor would like to continue to expand her range of angling experiences. "I usually manage to get somewhere every summer. And I am trying to maybe have one or two other experiences during the year." One possibility that intrigued her was salt water.

"Someday, I don't know when, it would be fun to do saltwater fishing for, what do you call it, the exciting fish in the shallow salt water? . . . The bonefish. I think it would be fun to try that. I like the trout fishing better, to be sure, but I would, before I hang up my fishing rod forever, like to at least try the bonefishing." She also would like to fish for snook.

When asked about her favorite angling companions, she again demurred on the details, for privacy and security reasons. "Well I have two or three good fishing friends and I don't think that it's appropriate to name them."

In 2009 President Barack Obama presented her with the Presidential Medal of Freedom, the United States' highest civilian award.

O'Connor has said that she wants her epitaph to read, "Here lies a good judge."

Chapter 13
Robert Rubin:
Budget Maven, Wall Street Whiz

As treasury secretary under President Bill Clinton, Robert Rubin's expertise in his métier – economics and finance -- enabled him to help plan and preside over the greatest peacetime economic expansion in the United States' history and lead the country to a balanced budget. Prior to his tenure as a public official, he was a hugely successful investment

Robert Rubin

analyst and manager for Goldman Sachs, one of the country's premier private financial firms. Not surprisingly, the skill and passion with which Rubin pursues his profession also characterize his approach to his favorite free-time pursuit: fly fishing.

Though he was born in New York City, Rubin moved with his family to Miami as a boy. Growing up near the Atlantic, Florida Bay, and the Keys in south Florida provided a natural segue to an interest in saltwater angling. "I used to go fishing with a spinning rod . . . we'd drive down to the Keys," Rubin said. Almost inevitably, however, other interests intervened after he graduated from high school. "I went away to college and law school and that kind of stuff and really never fished," he related.

Occasionally, highly accomplished and famous people, seemingly staid and stable pillars of gravitas from birth, surprise us with an uncharacteristic choice or act, a hearteningly spontaneous turn taken along their life path. Rubin, it seems, may be one.

According to a May 12, 1999, article on The BBC Online Network, after graduating *summa cum laude* from Harvard in 1960, Rubin reputedly left Harvard Law School after only three days to "see the world." Eventually he attended the London School of Economics and completed a law degree at Yale in 1964. He started his career as an attorney with a New York law firm and two years later joined Goldman Sachs' investment division.

In 1993 he joined President Bill Clinton's administration as White House economic adviser and was named treasury secretary in 1995, remaining until 1999. After leaving government he returned to Wall Street as an executive with Citibank. In a 2001 PBS interview, Rubin explained his reasons for leaving the lucrative world of Wall Street to serve the country.

"I'd wanted to be in government for as long as I could remember," he said, "and there were multiple reasons. I was exceedingly curious as to what the world looked like from inside the White

House, if one could have an appropriate job. And secondly, there were a lot of issues that I cared a lot about and was very interested in, and it seemed to me that there was no better way to pursue those than to be part of government -- once again, assuming that you had a job that kept you at the center of things, so that you actually had an effect."

Rubin has a career-long reputation for remaining calm and cerebral amid political and financial turmoil. In 2012 Bloomberg Businessweek's William D. Cohan wrote that "Rubin's knack for spreading wisdom and tranquility has been the defining trait of his professional life."

In 2004 he co-wrote the New York Times bestseller *In an Uncertain World: Tough Choices from Wall Street to Washington* with longtime Washington Post Company political journalist Jacob Weisberg. While this chapter was being finished Weisberg was chairman and editor-in-chief of the Slate Group. Business Week picked the book as one of 2004's top ten business books.

Rubin's long angling hiatus continued after he finished his studies and into his early working years. The long hours and taxing responsibilities of his nascent Wall Street career combined with starting a family dominated his life and he found no time for his boyhood hobby. But as he became established in his profession and his children grew up, he and his wife, Judith, began to make time for travel and relaxation; and fishing.

In studying literature, much is made about epiphanies, popular plot devices for developing characters. But on one of his trips with Judith, Rubin experienced a real-life version.

"Somewhere in the early 80s," he said, "I said to my wife, why don't we go to a place called Deepwater Cay that I read about, near Grand Bahama Island. It's kind of the ancestral bonefishing club. . . . So Judy and I went down. . . . And so we went out with a guide. She doesn't fish but we went out and I cast for bonefish (with a spinning rod). And we came back in and I saw somebody doing something else and I said what's he doing? And he (the guide) said, 'Oh, he's bonefishing just like you are.' I said, no he's not, it's something different. Well, he had a fly rod. So I said, gee that looks like really fun. Why can't I do that?" Rubin lost no time following up on his "discovery" and transforming his approach to his avocation.

"We got back to New York and I went over to an Orvis shop and I told them I had been bonefishing and I wanted to learn how to do that with a fly rod," he said. "So I bought a 9-weight and a 7-weight and I bought a Joan Wulff book on fly casting. . . . And I took the book home. We live in the city but we have a little house out in the country with a lawn big enough for this stuff. And I started learning from the book. And then I arranged with the guy who was a salesman at the Orvis shop to come by and give me some lessons. He has since become a world-famous guide. . . . This was 1983, roughly twenty-five years ago." Telling the story, Rubin paused for emphasis. "I have never fished with a spinning rod since. Never touched one." It did not take long for fly fishing to become his number one free-time pursuit.

In the more than thirty years since he first learned to fly fish, Rubin has availed himself of many opportunities. Like others of us, he has a Will Rogers outlook on fly fishing's limitless variety of fish species and destinations: He has never met one he did not like. When asked if he had a favorite place or kind of fly fishing he hesitated only a moment: "I really don't." He "loves" stalking Bahamas bonefish flats as much as casting to wild trout on the north fork of central Montana's Boulder River, where he owns a ranch with nine other partners. "Tom (Brokaw) has his own ranch up on the west branch, yeah, Tom McGuane's up there too," Rubin said. "But Brokaw's one of the ten in this thing. . . . and I love being up there. . . . I just love being on the water." Other Big Sky Country waters he has fished include the Ruby, the Madison, McCoy's Spring Creeks, Stodden

Slough, and the Beaverhead.

He reminisced about a camping trip into wild country he once made. "Five of us with outfitters and guides . . . hiked about three and a half hours into the back country of Yellowstone to fish Slough Creek, and I loved that," he said. "Fishing was very good. It's all cutthroat. . . . They each have their own strengths and weaknesses, but they are wonderful fish. I mean, I think rainbows are a more interesting fish, myself, but it's a wonderful fish." He also has traveled much farther afield. "I love Patagonia (in Chile and Argentina), but it's hard to get to," he said.

Like all highly successful people, Rubin faced time constraints throughout his career. "The only problem . . . is you've got to have a little bit of time. Because you've got to get on the water – it's not like playing tennis where you can play for an hour," he said.

Following his tenure as treasury secretary, Rubin became director and chairman of Citigroup, the international banking and financial firm. The job kept him so busy that it compressed his angling opportunities. Rubin adapted accordingly, traveling by helicopter – a forty-five minute flight instead of a two and a half hour drive by car -- to the West Branch of the Delaware River, near the New York-Pennsylvania border.

If he could get a couple of days, or sometimes just a day, he could go. His affection for the river practically in his backyard was evident. "I love the Delaware," he said. . . . It's a big river, which for the East is unusual, and they are wild fish, and sometimes they're big and they're very strong." He recalled a trip on which "I had about an eighteen- or nineteen-inch rainbow that took me into my backing."

With careful planning and time management, Rubin was able to stretch his angling horizons farther. If he could get two days off, he could go bonefishing. He acknowledged that he was more fortunate than most people because he could afford to "charter a little plane."

Once he had set aside the time, he would "go down in a night, fish the whole day, fish the next day, and go back." If he wanted a change from bonefishing he might head for the Everglades and the Ten Thousand Islands to pursue snook, redfish, and seatrout.

Like many other fly fishers, Rubin has found that myriad hours spent on the water have made him more environmentally conscious. While treasury secretary he one day observed a large area of dark brown in the Gulf of Mexico while flying to Palm Island in the Keys. When he asked the pilot about it he learned that it was an anoxic "dead zone," likely the result of too many nutrients being discharged into the waters from human activity.

At the time, state and federal officials were considering approval requests for a massive development project that had been proposed for the edge of the Everglades, near Miami. When he returned to Washington, Rubin contacted then Secretary of the Interior Bruce Babbit to ask his help in opposing the project. In the end, it was rejected. "I think I may have contributed a little bit to it (the rejection)," Rubin said.

Rubin fishes with a number of different friends, including former deputy treasury secretary Roger Altman and Peter Duchin, the renowned New York society pianist. Of Duchin, he said, "He's a fabulous fisherman. He grew up with it all his life."

Rubin, who was on the board of Ford Motor Company, has also fished with Ford Chairman Bill Ford at Blackberry Farm, a resort in the Great Smoky Mountains of Tennessee. But though they fished together only "once or twice," he said, "Every time we had a board meeting we talked about fishing."

Often, however, Rubin prefers to fish alone. "I go by myself quite a bit," he said. "If I go bonefishing I want to be with the guide by myself. I don't want anybody else in the boat. You know, you give up half your casts, and I don't want to do that. Then you lose your concentration."

He is proud of the fact that he is not a "goal-oriented angler," intent on racking up numbers and weights. And despite his obvious skills – a Montana guide friend of mine reported that he is "a *very* good trout fisherman" – Rubin is mildly self-critical. "My casting's fine, my line management's fine, I can read a river, that's all fine. I'm terrible in . . . figuring out which fly to use. So I either go with a guide or . . . or I let somebody get me six flies and say just try them until it works," he said.

In 2009 Rubin left Citigroup, a decision that seemed likely – even with his many other public and private obligations -- to free up more time for fly fishing. When this chapter was being written, among other responsibilities, Rubin co-chaired the Council on Foreign Relations and heaeds the community-development group the Local Initiatives Support Corporation. He was also a trustee at Mount Sinai Medical Center and the Harvard Corporation. Certainly there is no danger of his interest flagging. "I love being on the water, and I love reading about it, and I love doing it," he said.

According to my Montana friend, in 2012 Rubin caught an eight-pound brown on a dry fly while fishing a tributary of the Beaverhead River north of Dillon.

Chapter 14
Dick Cheney:
High Plains Drifter,
Rocky Mountain Wader

Talking with Dick Cheney about fly fishing, one is struck by the wistful reminiscences, quiet modesty, and dry humor so vastly out of synch with the former vice president's stereotypical media image as a hard-nosed political infighter. Cheney, speaking in an informal western vernacular – with occasional dropped G's on his gerunds and a few missing terminal R's – drew a compelling word picture of his life afield and astream.

Dick Cheney

Though born in the Midwest, there is no doubt that Cheney is a man of the Rockies and the High Plains. The two Western landscapes shaped his personality, his academic, government, and business careers, and his world view. And they especially fostered his enthrallment with his favorite pastime. Like most very good fly fishers, he served a long apprenticeship.

"In Nebraska when I first started (fishing) I was probably seven, eight years old, with a bamboo pole and a string and a worm," Cheney said. "I graduated to a spinning rod and hardware when we moved to Wyoming when I was thirteen." Though his parents and other relatives enjoyed the outdoors, as a boy there was no one to take him under their wing when it came to fly fishing.

"My family, Dad and Mom, were avid fishermen. . . . They loved to go out to Pathfinder Reservoir (near Casper) and set up a couple of chairs and throw the casting rod and the spinning rod out, but none of them fly fished," he said. The first leg of his mostly self-scripted journey to becoming an accomplished fly fisher began with a trip into the Bighorn Mountains with three high school friends.

"The summer I was sixteen we had summer jobs, we all played football, but then we took the week before football started and we went up on the middle fork of the Powder River," he said. "Clear up on top, at the south end of the Bighorns in Wyoming. There was a canyon up there. We parked up on top and every day we'd have to hike down into this horrendous deep canyon. A couple of the guys did fish, fly fish, but I got a second-hand fiberglass rod and a handful of flies at the local fly store, local hardware store," he said, correcting himself. "We didn't have a fly store in Casper. And that was the first time I'd ever used flies or a fly rod. The Middle Fork's a historic stream in Wyoming, but toward the headwaters a lot of boulders and pools and so forth. So there was no real serious fly casting, it was just to get your fly in the water. But that was the first time I'd ever done any fly fishing."

The experience stuck with him but events intervened. After high school he headed east to Yale University on a football scholarship. But in an episode that one suspects probably had a lot to do with homesickness, he flunked out. "Big transition going from small-town Wyoming to New Haven, Connecticut," he was quoted as saying by Biography.com.

After returning home, Cheney worked for a while as a lineman for a power company before enrolling at the University of Wyoming, in Laramie, earning a B.A. in political science in 1965 and a Master's degree in 1966. During his U of W years he also married Lynne Vincent, his high school sweetheart. Like many young couples starting a new life together, though poor in assets they were rich in hopes and dreams. He recalled the time fondly. And reconnected with fly fishing.

"I kept my rod under the bed," he said. "My wife and I lived in a furnished one-bedroom student housing apartment. Cost us forty-three dollars a month or something. I could get up early in the morning and drive up on the Snowy Range west of Laramie, within forty-five minutes of where we lived. And fish up there and catch a nice mess of fish and be back in time to make my morning classes."

Husband and wife moved on to doctoral programs at the University of Wisconsin, Madison. Lynne Cheney received a PhD in English but Dick dropped out before finishing his dissertation to take an intern's job in Washington on Wisconsin Congressman Bill Steiger's staff. The move marked the end of his academic career. Both academia and the move to D.C. hindered his fly fishing.

"I'd get a little bit of fishing in . . . in the summertime" Cheney said. "Didn't have a lot of money. And when I really got seriously engaged again was when I came back to Wyoming after I had worked for (President Gerald) Ford in the White House. In seventy-seven we came back out home and settled in to Casper, and I got curious about fly fishing again." The curiosity became an opportunity when, in 1978, he was elected Wyoming's congressional representative.

"The good thing about being congressman in Wyoming was you got to know where a lot of good fly water was," Cheney said. "A lot of those ranches had nice streams on them, and I used to travel with a fly rod in my car. And then I hired my home state rep who before he came to work for me was an outfitter. He had great connections around the state. So I got a lot of fishing done in those days. Because I'd be home traveling in the district, doing town hall meetings and holding office hours, making speeches and so forth, but you could always grab a few hours on various streams." Another fortuitous occurrence during his early congressional career exponentially improved his fly fishing skills.

"I met a great guy named Don Daugenbaugh. If I ever had a mentor, Don's it," Cheney said. "He was a schoolteacher and coach in Williamsport, Pennsylvania. And in the summertime he was a seasonal park ranger in Yellowstone, and that's part of my district. And I got to know him and we used to get together, he and I, and then this guy who worked for my home-state rep. For several years we'd meet in the big hotel in Yellowstone on Labor Day Weekend. This would have started in the early eighties, mid-eighties, eighty four, eighty-five. We'd rent a cabin up there for the weekend, and we'd fish basically the Yellowstone; Buffalo Ford, the famous waters in and around Yellowstone."

"Don was superb, the best fly fisherman I ever met," Cheney recalled. "The first time I went out with him I had an old bamboo rod that had been in my father-in-law's garage when we cleaned it out after he died. It was not a great bamboo fly rod, it was an old one and probably made in the twenties or thirties, and a spring-loaded reel with a lever on it. And that was great when you were catching panfish. But if you got a big one and it took a lot of line on you, it finally broke your reel, it just flew apart. Don watched me do that a couple of times on a couple of fish and he said, okay, first we're going to town to get you a decent fly rod. So we went in and I bought a Sage rod and reel, basically, and that's how I got equipped with modern equipment." His friendship with Daugenbaugh also bore other fruit back in the D.C. area.

"Don had a friend down about eight miles west of Gettysburg, a private stretch of water, there was a bunch of guys who had been going there for years and they had a cabin on it." Cheney remembered it as a "beautiful stream where they'd done a lot of work, big browns and brookies in it."

The annual Yellowstone rendezvous ended with Daugenbaugh's transfer to Fort Smith, in eastern Montana's High Plains. And Cheney was amazed to watch Daugenbaugh become an even better angler.

"He would fish the Bighorn about six days out of seven, do it better than any man I've ever seen," Cheney said. "So for many years we'd get together on the Bighorn. He had his own boat. He introduced me to something called a noodle rod, a ten-foot five-weight rod, whippy rod for nymphing really small nymphs, which is what you needed lots of times, fished deep on the Bighorn and that's where the big fish were. And if you used just regular gear they'd break you off in a minute. But that rod had so much play in it that once you hooked them, even on a 5X tippet, you had much better luck."

When we spoke, Cheney's memories of his Bighorn glory days with his mentor were tinged with a sense of regret at their ending because of Daugenbaugh's age and declining health. "I still keep up with Don but he's reached the point where he's on a walker," Cheney said. "He actually broke his hips, he's a World War II vet."

As Cheney's political career advanced, so did his fly fishing opportunities. "I also got involved in doing a lot more international stuff," he said. "I was secretary of defense eighty-nine to ninety-three (in President George Herbert Walker Bush's administration).

A lot of my hosts understood that I liked to fish. So I remember for example going to Chile on an official visit but the Chileans had me stay over a weekend. They flew me down to Punta Arenas, Chile, down at the tip of South America and they'd helicopter over to Tiera del Fuego. . . . I fished for the big sea-run browns."

The more exotic places he fished, the more it whetted his appetite. "And so as I got older and earned more money and could afford it I fished Argentina many times; San Martin de lo Sante, Tierra del Fuego; and New Zealand, Australia, the Ponoi in Russia. Steelhead in the Dean and in the Babine in British Columbia. For Atlantic salmon I fished the Restigouche, the Miramichi in New Brunswick. It got to the point where I was obnoxious. But I love it so, if I had one day to go that's how I'd want to spend it."

Among the many places Cheney fished was one that truly hooked him. "There's nothing better than fishing big steelhead on the Babine," he said. "We used to go up and stay, a bunch of us, and stay at the Silver Hilton there, the lodge, and when I got into all my heart difficulty here a few years ago I couldn't do that. I was approaching end-stage heart failure. The last time I went on the Babine would have been O-nine, the fall of O-nine. October was the slot we had up there, and I had reached the point where instead of being able to spend the day on the Babine, because you can't fish out of a boat, you know, you gotta wade, chest waders and big, fast water, so it was just more than I could handle physically."

The dark days of ill health had begun decades before – on the heels of a three-pack-a- day smoking habit -- with a heart attack at age thirty-seven. By the early teens of the new millennium, other cardiologic events over many years had grimly circumscribed Cheney's lifestyle and dangerously reduced his life expectancy. That all changed with one surgery.

"I got a heart transplant here about fifteen months ago," he said, his tone as exultant as one can expect from a laconic westerner. "It's amazing, only three years ago I was in end-stage heart failure, about to hang it up, and on an emergency basis one night they put a pump in my chest. That bought me twenty months and that got me on the transplant list and . . . the end of March last year, I got a new heart . . . so I'm back now."

"Back" means doing a lot more fly fishing. "I usually spend a lot of time along the south fork of the Snake along the Wyoming-Idaho border, my favorite stretch of water," he said. "Getting ready to go down here in a couple of weeks and fish the Green below Flaming Gorge. I haven't fished that for a long time. I've got trips planned later this year to the Miramichi, to the Bighorn back in Montana. There are a bunch of us, eight of us get together every year, we carve out a week and we do two days someplace else and then two days on an overnight float trip on the South Fork of the Snake. It's probably my home water to the extent that I've got any. We live right here within walking distance of it in Jackson Hole."

As all of us know, the love of fly fishing covers a wide swath. "Once you get into it, half the enjoyment comes when you're not even on the stream. Planning the trips, or figuring what flies to use," Cheney said. He lamented the fact that he never learned to tie. "I've got a beautiful kit, but I've never had time to use it," he said. "But getting organized, and the gear, and my wife keeps wondering how many fly rods a guy needs. To do it well it requires real concentration and is the kind of thing that when I'm out there on the water with my fly rod you don't worry about anything else, you're just focused on that."

He explained how that focus benefited his political career: "I got ready for my vice presidential debates, both in 2000 and 2004, we did a lot of preparation and drill and so forth but the day before the debate I went fishin'. . . . You've read the briefing books, you've read 'em all and the questions and the strategy and all the rest of it, and Rob Portman, senator now from Ohio, he was my debate opponent. I practiced against him both in 2000 and 2004, and he and I would head to the South Fork and spend the day on the river. That was the best way of all. You could relax and sort of clear out your head and that day of relaxation before the debate was a lot more valuable than trying to memorize answers to questions."

Instead of a dream trip he had not yet made, Cheney said, "I tend to think of the trips I'd like to go do again. The trip to the Ponoi was phenomenal, I took my daughter Mary with me, a good friend of mine who has since passed away. But we just had a magnificent time. . . . It's the best Atlantic salmon fishing I ever had."

Despite his love of salmon, steelhead top his favorite fish list. "You know, the first time I went fly fishing for steelhead I didn't catch a damn thing, fished all week," he said. "You gotta learn, obviously, and there is a lot to learn, in terms of presentation and so forth. And when you finally hook one it's a lifetime experience."

He is deeply grateful for his renewed good health. "I got to that point in life where first of all I thought it was about over then all of a sudden I get the gift of more years and I'm determined to use 'em to the best possible effect," he said. "I spend a lot of time with my grandkids and live in Jackson most of the year and spend a lot of time with my fly rods and my shotguns. . . . Yup, my biggest problem now is an old football knee."

When this chapter was written, his favorite fishing and bird hunting pal was fellow Cowboy Stater Dick Scarlett. "He's a banker here in Jackson," Cheney said. "Many years ago when I was trying to buy a house here in Jackson when I was just gettin' out of government, at one point Dick loaned me the money for a down payment on a house. Which I have always appreciated. . . . It's old Wyoming ties and connections."

Fly fishing tops Cheney's list of free time activities for reasons many of us share. "Well, you get to do it in some of the most beautiful places in the world," he said. "And it's hard to think of a time when I've met a fisherman you didn't want to spend time with. To do it well, obviously, you've really got to concentrate on it and work at it. And I'm sure there are a lot of other things like that, people paint or are into cars or whatever their pursuit may be, but it works for me and I think it works for a lot of others, too."

Though he had certainly not abandoned politics at the time we spoke, its pre-eminence in his life seemed to have faded. "I try to keep my head down, once in a while they make me mad and I have to sound off, about current affairs," he said. "But I'm very much enjoying the years. I'm grateful for the donor and the state of modern American medicine, and the prayers of a lot of people."

Chapter 15
John Hope Franklin:
Scholar, Civil Rights Pioneer

At ninety-two, John Hope Franklin was already looking forward to his next fly fishing vacation. Franklin, one of the country's most highly acclaimed academics (one hundred and thirty-seven honorary degrees), Civil Rights pioneer and recipient of the Presidential Medal of Freedom, helped guide the United States through one of the most wrenching periods in its history. In a sense, his name, his political philosophy, his profession, and his avocations – orchid culture and angling -- converged in one word: hope.

John Hope Franklin

Like most passionate fly fishers, Franklin, who was Professor Emeritus of American History at Duke University, began his angling apprenticeship at an early age with the pursuit of quainter, more basic methods. He first learned from his mother when he was eight years old and living in the tiny village of Rentiesville, Oklahoma. It was 1923 and because his father was living and practicing law sixty-five miles away in Tulsa, keeping him away from his family sometimes for weeks at a time. In his autobiography, *Mirror to America*, Franklin recounted his mother's efforts to compensate for her husband's long absences.

"Mother strove to engage me in pastimes she thought young boys would like," Franklin wrote. "Thus, she taught me how to fish. We would dig for worms after a rain and keep them until the spare Saturday morning or holiday. She could take a straight sapling and trim and polish it down to a fishing pole as well as anyone. Our line was heavy thread or light string, and the only concession we made to manufacturers was in the purchase of hooks. We were on a serious mission when we went to Elk Creek and cast out our line for sun perch or catfish, intent on taking home our dinner."

In our conversation, Franklin wondered what his mother would think about his catch-and-release fly fishing ethic, when some days he returned to the water trout "that could have fed the three of us for two days."

Franklin recalled how he fell in love with fly fishing forty-three years before, while he was a visiting professor at Cambridge University, in England.

"I was talking big around the colleges about in England you had to be a descendent of William the Conqueror or King John before you could qualify to fish, in England anyway, and that word got around," he recalled. "So this fella at the college said to me in the fall of 1963, 'I say Franklin, do you fancy fishing?' "

"I said, 'Yeah but I can't fish here,' and then I put on my spiel that you had to be privileged and well born and the rest of it. And he said, 'I don't know as that's always true, but I think that if you'd like to fish I can lay it on.' "

The "fella" was another professor, John Raven, whose home was near Oban, in Western Scotland. "About two or three weeks later a note came from him," Franklin continued. "It said, 'Dear Franklin, if you would be at the King's Cross Station and take the night train to Oban, Scotland, on the eighteenth of June – this was ten months later, you see – and there'll be some other chaps there who'll be coming up. . . . Meet those chaps and maybe you'll have dinner together and the next morning be sure to get off in Oban, and have a look around the town, it's an interesting town."

Throughout the long months of waiting, Raven and Franklin kept in touch frequently. "I would run into him during the winter and spring, at Cambridge, and he would say, 'Is everything laid on, Franklin?' and I said yes. And so it turned out just as he said. There were two men on the train and I looked them up and we had dinner together and had a nice time. . . . One was director of the Cambridge College Choir and the other was the director of the Cambridge University Press. And we got along very well." The other men had both been regular angling guests of Raven but Franklin was unsure what to expect and too self conscious to ask.

Upon their arrival, Raven met the men and drove them to his home. Franklin, who knew Raven only as a fellow academic, was stunned when the party arrived at the Raven family's fifty-thousand-acre ancestral estate, Ardtornish. Soon he was shown into his room, complete with private bath, in the "baronial castle."

When it came time to prepare for fishing, Raven took Franklin to his gear storage area. "I saw his fly rods racked up in the garage and I said one day I'm going to have rods like that," Franklin said. "Meanwhile, I didn't *realize* they were fly rods. I didn't know fly fishing. I think he suspected that, that I couldn't fish with flies. So when I began to unwrap my fly rod he began to look at me out of the corner of his eye and he said, 'I say Franklin, you may need a little help.' Well, I needed a lot of help, because I didn't know what the hell I was doing."

"The reason I suspected that he had some suspicion about that was that the man who managed his farms . . . was there with him. And he just said to him, 'Would you help Franklin a little bit.' And so this man, who fly fished like an angel, and I couldn't even un-wrap the line, he just stood by me and helped me. . . . He stayed with me for about ten days . . . and taught me all I know about fly fishing, which is not too much, still," he recalled, chuckling.

"I wasn't so successful (one sea bass)," he continued, "but nei-ther was anyone else in the party. . . . There were Glasgow business-men who . . . paid him (Raven) fifty pounds per week per rod, and they didn't catch anything either." Despite its being a far cry from the salmon they were pursuing, Franklin's catch was dutifully re-corded and described in the estate's log book. Fondly reminiscing four decades later, Franklin recalled John Raven's wife, Faith, who "could fly fish like a ballet dancer. She didn't fish that first time," he remembered, "but I saw her later several times."

Despite this inauspicious introduction to the sport, the interlude began Franklin's love affair with fly fishing that intensified over the decades. For a quarter century he headed west every July to pursue the "marvelous browns and rainbows" of Montana's Madison River. Every year he planned his vacation around the annual pilgrimage.

Franklin's life story is a profile in courage, commitment, a love of learning, and trailblazing accomplishment marked by a duality of purpose: pursuing scholarly excellence – both as a university pro-fessor and a prolific author -- and fighting for social justice.

Born into the toxic social atmosphere of racial hatred in the South in 1915, in his early years he lived through the murderous 1921 race riots in Tulsa, the privations of the Depression, and the crushingly dehumanizing system of de jure segregation.

Early on he developed a passion for learning that was to set the course for his life, developing it into a rigorous scholarly quest, first as an undergraduate at Fisk University, then Harvard, where he earned a PhD in History. Within a few short years after getting his doctorate, Franklin was one of the United States' foremost historians and a highly sought after professor.

He wrote or edited nearly a score of books, including the definitive history of African Americans *From Slavery to Freedom*, which has sold more than three and a half million copies since its publication in 1947. An indefatigable freedom fighter, Franklin stood shoulder to shoulder (figuratively and literally) with other giants of the Civil Rights movement: Thurgood Marshall, Martin Luther King, Jr., Ralph Bunche, and others. His activism included participation in the iconic 1965 march from Selma to Montgomery, Alabama, and battling for enactment of the federal Civil Rights Act and the Voting Rights Act.

Franklin's academic career took him to some of the world's most prestigious universities. From 1964 to 1970 he was a member (and chairman the last three years) of the Department of History at the University of Chicago, where he lived around the corner from fellow professor Norman Maclean. Ironically, neither knew the other fly fished.

"We would walk to school together," Franklin recalled. "Norm didn't know that I fished. We never talked about it. I did not know until I moved away from Chicago and I read *A River Runs Through It* that he was one of the great fly fishermen."

"It's a great story," he added of the book (and subsequent movie) that spawned a fly fishing revolution.

As we talked, he said he did not have a dream trip in mind. "Just to go back to the Madison one more time. It's my idea of ideal fishing." His two-and-a half decade routine was interrupted only once, by the death of his wife, Aurelia, in 1999.

When it came to flies, his tastes were eclectic: Grasshoppers, Wooly Buggers, Cadisses, nymphs, wet flies. This sparked arguments with his best fishing buddy. "He thinks wets are disreputable," Franklin said, chuckling. "Sometimes if they're not taking a dry fly, our guide will insist that he put on a wet fly. And he will do it with great reluctance . . . . But I'll fish with anything."

Since his Scotland foray more than four decades earlier, part of fly fishing's appeal for Franklin was as a respite from the hurly burly of public obligations, book deadlines, and academic duties. "I think it has had a profound effect on me, outlook and so forth," he said. But he also compartmentalized it. "I don't get inspiration for my books by fishing, or vice versa. . . . I'm after that fish. I'm not thinking about teaching or about a book, unless it's a book that will tell me more about how to get that fish," he said.

Despite his love of fly fishing, Franklin still harked back to his angling roots. "I never fully got away from the way my mother taught me," he said. "And though I don't fish with quite the crude, undeveloped way when I was seven or eight years old, I still like to fish with a spinning rod and reel and live bait, lures. I still enjoy that. . . . I've never given it up."*

*John Hope Franklin died at the age of 93, during the writing of this book.

Chapter 16
Rick Porcello:
Worthy Successor
To Cy Young, Ted Williams

If there is one baseball team most closely associated with fly fishing, it is the Boston Red Sox. This link originates with Baseball Hall of Famer Ted Williams, acknowledged as the best hitter of all time (even by Joe DiMaggio) and the last man to hit .400 in a season (.406 in 1941). As great a hitter as he was, Williams by his early

Norm Zeigler

thirties was also one of the world's top fly fishers. Many of us grew up reading stories in the outdoor magazines of his adventures in New Zealand, New Brunswick, the Florida Keys, and other exotic destinations. In fact, for this fly fisher, the tales of Williams' exploits chasing trout, salmon, tarpon, bonefish and other species around the world became one of the seminal reasons for wanting to pursue the sport.

These days there is a new Red Sox player in Boston to carry on Williams' tradition of combining excellence in baseball and fly fishing – right-handed power pitcher Rick Porcello, winner of the 2016 American League Cy Young award.

Like Williams, Porcello approaches the game with toughness, fierce dedication and exceptional skill.

When Porcello takes the mound it is unambiguously clear to opposing batters -- even those who have never batted against him – that

they are facing a daunting opponent. Besides his deadly sinking fastball and an outstanding seven-year record in Major League Baseball with the Detroit Tigers and the Sox, there is the fact that Porcello could have been picked by central casting to play a dominating pitcher.

At six feet five and two hundred and five workout-toughened pounds, with cable-taut forearms and a deceptively placid mien, there is no mistaking his intention: to mow down the hitter and send him angry and dejected back to the dugout. The same drive and intensity of a world-class athlete -- though not the relentless competitiveness -- mark Porcello's approach to fly fishing.

Growing up in Chester Township, New Jersey, Porcello spent plenty of time exploring the outdoors as well as playing organized sports. Fishing has been part of his life nearly as far back as he can remember. But his fly fishing pursuits started one Christmas when he and his two brothers, Zach and Jake, found fly rods under the tree. "I was ten or twelve," he said. At that time no one in the family was a fly fisher and there would be no formal instruction.

"When we got those fly rods . . . we kind of learned on our own," he said, though they also consulted a few books. As with any new outdoors pursuit – i.e. skiing, ice skating, off-road biking -- the learning itself brought fun and discovery, prompting outings to local ponds and streams, some of them tiny and unnamed back-yard waters and others better-known, such as the Raritan River. But Porcello's intense infatuation with fly fishing truly began when the family acquired a vacation house in Vermont a stone's throw from the Deerfield River. Even today he thinks of it as his home water, fondly reminiscing about memorable dry fly outings and big browns that hit swung streamers.

Queried about his favorite kind of fly fishing he recounted, "I basically grew up with dry flies and streamers," on trout streams. And although his travels in the last decade and a half have broad-ened his angling opportunities – partly because of his peripatetic profession -- he has never lost his love of his early pursuits. Still, he admits, "I think it has evolved." He has pursued steelhead in the up-per Midwest and on the West Coast (Oregon's Grand Ronde River), caught striped bass in New England, and boated tarpon, snook, and redfish in Florida.

At the same time he was becoming a skilled fly fisher – during his teens – Porcello was also maturing into an exceptional multi-sport high school athlete. He credits a high school coach with giving him a leg up to the Major Leagues by persuading him in his junior year to drop the other team sports and focus on baseball. Following that advice paid off almost immediately as it became evident that Porcello was a brilliantly talented pitcher with skills far above his age class. Playing for Seton Hall Prep in 2007, his senior year, his win-loss record was 10-0 with 103 strikeouts and a 1.44 ERA. He also pitched a perfect game. His accomplishments on the mound put him at the head of the 2007 Major League draft class.

Though he had locked up a scholarship at the University of North Carolina, Porcello decided to forgo college baseball and jump straight to the pros. After being picked by the Detroit Tigers, he spent seven years with the team before being traded to the Red Sox in December 2014.

Serendipitously, the Sox's Fort Myers, Florida, spring training facility – officially named Jet Blue Stadium but affectionately known as Fenway South – is only twenty miles from a world-class saltwater fly fishing destination: Sanibel Island and its surrounding waters. Soon after showing up at the Southwest Florida training site in February 2015 Porcello was exploring the region with his fly rod and hooking up snook, redfish, seatrout and other species around the island. About a year later he bought a house in nearby Naples, along with a flats boat and trailer that he keeps in the garage.

Porcello – his full name is Frederick Alfred Porcello III -- is in some ways an atypical twenty-first century pro athlete. Modest and taciturn, flash and notoriety are not his style. He does not travel with a retinue of hangers-on (aka "posse") and prefers time alone or with his brothers or a friend exploring new angling retreats over mingling with brash crowds in rowdy party hangouts.

As for many of us, his thoughts go beyond the fish. "I think there are probably many lessons that can be learned in fly fishing," he said. For him, he explained, the work you put into it directly affects your success and progress. You learn patience and persistence and self control. "I relate that to my baseball career," he said. "It takes work at the start."

Still, for him fly fishing "is always relaxing, especially in pro ball." In a sense, he was referring not only to the stresses of the game itself but also to the asceticism and self-discipline adopted by some of the most successful professional athletes to help them perform at their peaks. Porcello follows a diet recommended by the Red Sox's team nutritionist and takes off only two weeks a year for relaxation. The rest of the time he maintains a self-imposed fitness regimen that includes weight training, running, and other beneficial workout schemes.

When the first hint of Florida spring shows itself, he is among the earliest arrivals at Fenway South, well before the mandatory reporting date for pitchers and catchers. In this period his schedule is simple: workouts weekday mornings, fly fishing afternoons and weekends.

Befitting a young man's dreams – he was not yet thirty when this was written -- Porcello's fly fishing bucket list is long and eclectic: Belize for permit and bonefish, New Zealand for giant trout. He wants to catch arctic char and Atlantic salmon; and to sight fish for tarpon on the Keys' flats. Among his free-time pursuits, fly fishing is "number one by far. It is my absolute favorite," he said

In addition to his angling aspirations, Porcello is also part of the longstanding thoughtful fly fishing tradition that goes far beyond gear, tactics, and catching fish. "You start to understand how human beings can impact the environment," he said. He supports strong protections for fisheries and habitat. He also takes care to make the small, individual gestures: pulling monofilament tangles out of mangroves, and picking up cans, plastic bags and other detritus in the water or along the shore.

Major League Baseball's grueling schedule, which with spring training and playoffs can last up to nine months, looks daunting to an outsider. It would seem to almost preclude other activities. But Porcello makes the best of it, fitting his fly fishing into a compressed time frame. "If I get to fish maybe a half dozen times in the season . . . I probably fish fifty to seventy-five days a year," he said.

Many of us realize that most of life is anticipation and memories, that a moment of experience is fleeting and evanescent. Building fly fishing memories becomes one of the sport's great joys. Porcello also understands this concept well. "I've been really lucky to have some memorable fish," he said. He recalled a steelhead that smashed his streamer as it swung down and behind a large rock on the Grand Ronde.

"One of the coolest, most memorable fish" was a brown trout he stalked on the Deerfield River. The fish was repeatedly rising near a tall-grass bank and a rainbow trout was rising very near it. He dropped his dry fly right on top of the rainbow so it would move away but it took the fly and he landed it. After releasing the rainbow he saw that the brown was still rising, pushing its big nose up through the river's surface tension every few seconds. In what is always one of fly fishing's most gratifying moments, he made a perfect cast diagonally upstream, landing the fly softly a short drift above the fish.

After a jolting take and a thrash-and-run fight, when the fish was brought to hand he could exult, "It was probably an eighteen to twenty-inch brown, just a beauty," he said. "With all its spots it was like a leopard brown."

As a lifelong Red Sox fan, it is a fine feeling to know that Rick Porcello has a lifetime of great pitches, and memorable fish, in his future.

Chapter 17
Patrick Hemingway:
Heir to Intellect and Wanderlust

It is probably a safe bet to say that – especially in the mid twentieth century -- not too many people chose to go from a magna cum laude degree in literature from Harvard to the life of a safari operator, game ranger, and wildlife official in eastern Africa. But Patrick Hemingway is cut from a different mold than the stereotypical Ivy Leaguer.

Ernest Hemingway Collection, John F. Kennedy
Presidential Library and Museum, Boston

Hemingway, the last surviving son of Nobel Prize winning author Ernest Hemingway, has been an avid outdoorsman all his life. Growing up in Key West and Cuba and making vacation trips to the Rockies with the family, he absorbed his father's adventurous spirit and passion for fishing, hunting and other active outdoor pursuits. In his 1969 book *Ernest Hemingway: A Life Story,* biographer Carlos Baker wrote that during a July 1936 interlude at the L-Bar-T ranch near Cook City, Wyoming, Ernest remarked that "in the first twelve hours Patrick had stayed off his horse only long enough to eat." Patrick was all of eight years old.

Like his father, Patrick Hemingway's grit and toughness are an integral part of his life and personality, though in a more introspective way. At the time this chapter was written he was in his eighties and was touting the benefits of wet wading the Missouri River as a palliative for post-hip replacement surgery. His conversations were punctuated by a spontaneous, infectious laugh, often occasioned by anecdotes about his own foibles.

Not surprisingly, fishing (though not fly fishing) played a big part in his Key West childhood. He recalled it fondly. "The fishing I did on the Keys was before people started to do it (saltwater fly fishing). In those days you used live crabs and live shrimp," he said. "And I'm telling you, catching a permit with a live crab is one of the easiest things on earth. . . . Because the permit hunts by scent. That's why it's so difficult to get on a fly."

In Wyoming, he recalled, "We bait fished with grasshoppers when we were young. . . on the L-Bar-T . . . there on the Clark Fork of the Yellowstone. In those days, at least where we were fishing, it was a cutthroat stream. And my dad and my mother used to fish it with two flies, wet flies, a McGinty and something else. Those cutthroat would eat anything." But though he observed his parents fly fishing, he first learned it himself in his late teens.

"It was right after the end of World War II . . . probably . . . in the summer of 1946, '47," he said, "because my older half brother, Jack, was just out of the service. And my mother had managed to get one of the very first Fords to come off of the assembly line after the war. . . . And Jack more or less took us around to the areas that he'd become familiar with just before the start of the war, when he was a late teenager."

"And so we took off from Florida and we drove all the way and I think the first thing that we went to was Dan Bailey's Fly Shop in Livingston. It was a sort of a beacon of light in an otherwise pretty fly shopless world. And we got a bunch of flies there, mostly dry flies, and we fished in Yellowstone Park. Jack really acted as our instructor and introduced us to all of the knots and stuff like that, and we fished the Firehole and the Gibbon. And then . . . the next place I remember is we were over on the road that parallels the Columbia River and we fished the river that comes off of Mount St. Helens." (Probably the North Fork of the Toutle River.)

"It was on the north side of the Columbia, and that was where my brother Jack got his first steelhead. . . . I remember we were down on the lower part of the river and he went further up the river and he came back with . . . an enormous fish from the standpoint of trout. . . . And he was pretty pleased with himself."

Soon after, Hemingway left Key West for Stanford University, staying one year before transferring to Harvard. His Africa years were dominated by the blood sports he loved most. "My greatest interest is shooting, I mean hunting," he said. "Of course the Brits don't like you to refer to 'hunting,' but I really like big game hunting, bird hunting, you know, those are the things that mean the most to me." Close behind is fly fishing. Interestingly, even in Africa he was able to pursue all three, since one of the positive remnants of British colonial days was the trout they brought with them.

Hemingway fly fished in some legendary and seemingly unlikely places. "In southern Tanzania there were a few streams that had been stocked in the southern plateau area. . . . That (when he fished them) would have been in the '60s," he said. "And those were stocked with brown trout, as I remember. . . . And I fished a little bit in the Kenya highlands, too."

The likelihood of encountering dangerous wildlife in most areas where he fished was slim. "In that area (southern Tanzania), that was mostly sort of dairy farms, pretty much like England, you know. Because the areas where you had trout were usually in highland areas and cattle areas," he said. One exception was certain areas around Mount Kenya.

"I fished also in the seventies on Kilimanjaro," he continued. . . . A twelve-inch fish was a big deal. But they were fun to fish, I mean tiny, little streams. . . . There were quite a lot of rainbows."

"The trouble with all of that African fishing is there was a kind of plentiful source of plant poison that you could use. And the natives got onto them pretty well and so they would poison the fish and get them. . . . An angler might travel to a favorite stream and find that all the fish had been killed out."

"I don't know how well the fishing in east Africa, the trout fishing, has held up," he said with wistfulness for a distant time and place. "I just have not heard any reports on it."

During his Africa years, Hemingway's fly fishing was sporadic. But that changed dramatically when he returned to the United States and moved to Montana. He referred to his early years in Bozeman as his "re-introduction" to the sport.

"When I came back, retired from working in Africa in 1975, I really wanted to take up fly fishing because, you know, it's the thing to do in the West. . . . I was very keen to really re-vamp and learn about it. And I had difficulties because so many of the people I met talked great fly fishing but when you actually went out with them they didn't really know anything. So it was hard to separate the real people who knew. . . . And I was lucky to meet some really great fishing friends. Most of them now are dead." One of them was John Bientendeufel.

"He was one of the real Pennsylvania fly fishermen, that really cut his teeth on those spring creeks in Pennsylvania," Hemingway said. "I think he'd been a corpsman in the Navy and then he got a football scholarship to MSU, and then he went back (East). He majored in economics, and his first job was with the Morgan Bank in Pittsburgh, mostly, you know, visiting default loan people. He decided he really didn't like that life too much and he moved out to Montana. . . . He was a wonderful type, and really a fine fisherman."

He also fished again with Jack; often. "He was very kind to me," Hemingway recalled of his half brother, who died in 2000. "He took us to a lot of his fishing places. . . . We had a wonderful trip to Henry's Lake in the late fall one time, that's when Henry's Lake is very fishable with surface streamers."

Another time they traveled to the Blackfoot Indian Reservation in northwest Montana. "He . . . tied up a bunch of scuds on a tippet where you had one scud after another separated by about an inch," Hemingway recalled. "And you had about eight scuds in a row. This lake up on the reservation was surrounded by a weed bed on the edge, and with conventional flies it was hopeless, but you could drag this scud thing through the weeds and the fish would take it. And I'm telling you, he was a much better fisherman than I am, and that afternoon he must have gotten at least ten fish over five pounds."

Hemingway showed no hesitation when queried about his favorite kind of angling. "The type of fly fishing that I enjoy very much is traditional dry fly fishing," he said. "I've never cared much for nymph fishing. I call it fly fishing with a worm, or worm fishing with a fly. . . . Now, I'm a very good streamer fisherman, and I learned to do that in Chile. . . . And so, I can really bash a streamer all day long. I like the thrill of the take on a streamer, but I really enjoy classic dry fly fishing."

In salt water he has boated yellowfin tuna, dolphin and jacks on flies.

When it came to his favorite fly fishing place, however, the answer came more slowly. "Well, it's hard to say, all these places. . . . I feel that I'm coming to the end of my fishing career. The age at which you are has a lot to do with it."

On further consideration he picked the Missouri River near his second home in Craig, Montana, where he and his wife, Carol, spend part of each year. "Over the years it's been wonderful. . . . I would say that fishing the Missouri River, say, ten years ago was the golden age for me," he said.

Hemingway is a more cerebral fly fisher than most. His knowledge and opinions about the sport tend toward the eclectic, erudite, and iconoclastic.

"I think fly fishing appeals to the more precise professions – diplomats, bankers, accountants – it's not your red-blooded, knock-'em-out types," he said.

As an example he cited British Foreign Secretary Lord Grey of Fallodon, who insisted on honoring Britain's commitment to Belgium's neutrality at the beginning of World War I.

"He wrote a number of books," Hemingway said. "One of the most famous was *The Charm of Birds*. . . . And he had a fishing hut on the Test. . . . and he also wrote the book, I think it's called *Fly Fishing*. He's one of the more important people in modern history because if England had not declared war on Germany in the First World War I think the history of the world would've been very different."

"He, of course, went blind," Hemingway said. "And his description in his book on fly fishing on what it meant to go blind and how it affected his fishing is very moving."

Hemingway draws connections between fly fishing and more arcane disciplines. When we spoke he had taken a strong interest in meteorology. "I've come very late to the subject and I find that vector analysis is not easy for me," he said, "but I really enjoy very vigorous intellectual pursuits. And one thing about fly fishing is . . . it's quite interesting from the standpoint of what underlies so much of meteorology, which is the study of fields. The behavior of a dry fly on a moving river gives you a lot of insight into fluid dynamics."

Part of fly fishing's appeal, he said, is that it imparts "a certain delicacy, interest in what animals and what fish actually do. And I think it leads you on to be interested in the biology of fish. . . . You know, one of the most interesting statements in the fly fishing literature is Vince Marinaro wrote a statement about the trout: 'Contrary to popular belief, the trout is a very stupid animal.'. . . The thing is, they are hard wired, you know, and the way they react to taking their food and so forth, people don't realize that we are much smarter than most of the animals we deal with."

In addition to sharing his encyclopedic knowledge, Hemingway is also not reticent about expressing his opinions. "I have come to dislike certain fly fishermen," he said. "The ones that are . . . so well clothed . . . and really come to regard it as a religion that makes them superior to other people. . . . I've never really liked the idea of making it into a religion or a lifestyle."

"And I've never believed in catch and release. I consider catch and release a necessity (for fisheries preservation), but I believe in killing fish and eating them. I love trout. And I know how to cook them. And I know how to clean them as well," he said. The best fish for the pan, he said, are sea-run cutthroats, which he described as "a sort of miniature version of the Atlantic salmon as far as the way it tastes. And I always make a joke that even the most religiously dedicated catch-and-releaser keeps the sea-run cutthroat."

He still revels in new angling experiences, such as his serendipitous "discovery" of wet wading. "It's almost like having an icepack. It does away with any of the soreness. And of course, Archimedes' Principle, it sort of supports you."

For him, there is no doubt about the origins of his love for the outdoors. "I think I got it very much from him (Ernest)," he says. "It's hard to say, because no matter where people are born they gravitate to certain things. And I think I would have been an out-doorsman even without a father. But I certainly got a head start."

Ironically, Hemingway never actually fly fished with his father. "The closest we came to that was with my stepmother, Mary, and so it wouldn't have been too long after World War II, and we were all getting together for that summer and going to be in Sun Valley," he said. "But she had this terrible health crisis, one of those fallopian (ectopic) pregnancies and this took place in Wyoming, in Casper, and so she was in the house recovering from this and we came out and stayed with my Dad and there was a fellow named Blackie, I can't remember his last name, who took us down to the – you call it the miracle mile there – it's the Platte River."

In his ninth decade, Hemingway still dreamed of new fly fish-ing challenges, of following the wanderlust in his genes to distant waters. "I'd like to fish in the Straits of Magellan," he said. "The farthest south I got in Chile is Coihaique. The port there is Aisen and then you can drive in to Coihaique, which is fairly close to the Argentine border. And that lake is Patagonia, but it's not the same as fishing farther south there, where you fish the actual channel."

Chapter 18
Paul J. Weitz:
"THE RIGHT STUFF"
for Space and Streams

There is no question that former Navy pilot, Shuttle and Skylab astronaut Paul J. Weitz is an all-American hero. But speaking to this reserved, low-key man one could get the impression that he is merely another comfortably ensconced retiree who stepped out of the ordinary, workaday world. Weitz, who recounts his extraordinary careers flying jets and spacecraft in a laconic, matter-of-fact manner,

National Aeronautics and Space Administration

was one of the people whose skill, daring, and bravery epitomized Tom Wolfe's era of Space Age giants imbued with the "RIGHT STUFF." And with his calm, competent demeanor it seems natural to presume that he is exactly the kind of man comrades and colleagues would want beside them in an aerial dogfight or on a crucial space mission.

Even as a boy growing up in northwestern Pennsylvania, Weitz wanted to be a Navy pilot in the tradition of his dad, who served in World War II. The times, the landscape, and family ties – an uncle who was an inveterate outdoorsman -- infused his boyhood with a penchant for active outdoor pursuits, especially hunting and fishing. After high school he attended Penn State, graduating with a BS in aeronautical engineering while earning his Navy commission through the university's ROTC program. But because he was first assigned to ship duty for a year after college, it was more than two years later that he earned his pilot's wings. A decade after his bachelor's he earned a master's degree in aeronautical engineering from the Navy's postgraduate school in Monterey, California.

With the Vietnam war raging, Weitz flew numerous combat missions over Southeast Asia, eventually racking up more than six thousand hours' flight time in jets before retiring. Among his many awards for service and bravery throughout his Navy career were the Distinguished Service Medal, the Air Medal, the Navy Commendation Medal, and the Los Angeles Chamber of Commerce Kitty Hawk Award.

Twelve years into his Navy service – in April 1966 -- Weitz was one of a new cohort of nineteen pilots and scientists picked by the National Aeronautics and Space Administration to join the astronaut corps. NASA was in its heyday, with the Apollo program entering its final, critical phase of sending men to the moon and back, and the agency was also gearing up to launch an orbital laboratory (Skylab) and, eventually, to segue into the Shuttle era. Weitz was in the thick of the space agency's projects, including a tentative assignment to command one of the later moon missions.

Skylab's launch in mid-April 1973 became both an opportunity and a risk for Weitz and his two other astronaut colleagues when NASA discovered that the flight into orbit had damaged some of the laboratory's critical components. The spacecraft's two solar power cells had not extended and a micrometeorite/sun shield had been torn away. The damage threatened to destroy the lab. After postponing the crew's rendezvous flight for several weeks, NASA launched Weitz and his colleagues on May 25 with tools, replacement parts, and instructions it hoped would save Skylab.

In what one historical account called a case of good old American "can-do" spirit, Weitz and his team were able to salvage and repair the orbiting laboratory, despite the fact that the repairs went very differently from the ones planned by on-the-ground engineers. During the repair process, Weitz and his two colleagues, Captain Charles "Pete" Conrad, Jr. and Commander Joseph P. Kerwin, revived the Skylab program with their ingenuity and marathon tethered space walks, installing a sun shield and tugging the solar panels into functional positions. Without their efforts the lab would have functionally self destructed from overheating and lack of electrical power.

The Skylab crew went on to perform a plethora of scientific experiments, including recording a solar flare from space and providing data on weightless environments' effects on the human body. They also set a then record for hours in space, with six hundred and seventy-two.

Weitz had lost the chance for a moon flight – he had been scheduled for the Apollo 20 mission -- when the program was shut down in December 1972 after Apollo 17, in what every astronaut who has spoken publicly about it has called a huge blunder.

After Skylab, it would be ten years before he returned to space in 1983, that time as commander on the first flight of the Space Shuttle

Challenger. Eventually he assumed more down to earth duties as deputy director of Houston's Johnson Space Center, a position he held until his 1994 retirement.

When this chapter was written, Weitz and his wife, Suzanne, had been living in Flagstaff, Arizona, for nearly two decades. As with many other people who pursue high-powered careers with big-time responsibilities, it took retirement to provide time for his becoming an accomplished fly fisher.

"I did some fly fishing when I was in my teens back in Pennsylvania," Weitz said, "but didn't really know what I was doing, so I didn't really pick up fly fishing until I had retired and moved here to Flagstaff." In a logical move for a scientist and military man, instead of blundering ahead on his own, at age sixty-two he joined a local fly fishing club and signed up for casting instruction at a Phoenix area fly shop. Though he did not grow up with the advantage of a fly fishing dad, long dormant memories of days astream with his uncle in the Keystone State piqued his interest in again taking up the sport. The love of nature that is part and parcel of fly fishing also prompted him to become an avid birder. Most central to his post-career outdoor life, Weitz said, has been Lees Ferry in far northern Arizona along the Utah border.

The fifteen mile long stretch of the Colorado River below Glen Canyon Dam, sometimes called Lees Reach, is touted by a local fly shop as "The World's Largest Spring Creek." This tailwater trout fishery, created by the reliably clear, cold flow coming from the depths of Lake Powell, is an example of man's sometimes positive transformational power over nature. It is managed by the Arizona Game and Fish Department as a blue-ribbon trout water.

Weitz makes the trip with different fishing pals six or eight times a year, staying three or four days at a time. "I'll be going up there in a couple of weeks to do that," he remarked. "It's handy. Lee's Ferry's only two hours away."

Closer to home are less glamorous but more easily reachable fly fishing opportunities. "We do have some converted stock tanks in this area, within fifty to a hundred miles, that have been converted into fisheries by Game and Fish with the help of the lessee," Weitz said. "Most of this land, you know, is National Forest and it's leased a lot for grazing. So we do make forays that way." Though the fish – rainbows -- are not wild or indigenous, they provide the bend in the rod that every fly angler seeks.

"And another favorite place is on the San Juan River below Navaho Dam," he continued. "That's in the far northern part of the state, it practically butts on the Colorado border. That's another tail-water, so we do that, and it has some big fish and it is absolutely a great fishery up there. It's technical fishing and I don't catch a lot of fish when we I go there. But it's a nice place, it's a nice stretch of river."

Weitz and his friends prefer to wade rather than fish from a boat. "There's a lot of guided trips in float boats but most of it is done, a lot of fishing is done wading'" he said. "The San Juan there is not as large a river as the Colorado. Typical flows in that region are, you know, five hundred to a thousand cfs (cubic feet per second). At the widest part of the wadeable area maybe. Well there's one section there, it's not all fishable, the water is probably three hundred yards wide, and the fishable water is a hundred to a hundred and fifty yards wide. Good size. Course that's not where the best fishing is."

In an acknowledgement of the San Juan's popularity, Weitz's advice to anglers was not to go there for the solitude but for the fishing. As with the Colorado, annually he makes a half dozen or more trips to the area with friends.

The fish can be large, but for him generally not huge. "About a year or two ago I guess I caught about a sixteen-inch brown," he said. "And then about ten minutes later I had on one I lost, it was a big rainbow and when it jumped the last time I saw it, it was at least that big, also, in the same place. So they have a good mix of browns and rainbows in there, although it's predominantly browns."

Weitz also occasionally travels to Colorado. "As a matter of fact, I fished the Frying Pan three weeks ago (we were talking in mid-May). The fishing was not very good at all," he said, "and the weather was even worse (snow and rain). The older guys that I go with, I said I'm not going in early May anymore. The weather around Basalt is just too changeable that time of year."

Because the Frying Pan is also a tailwater, the problem was not that the river was blown out. "No, it wasn't high water," he said. "As a matter of fact they had just increased the flow to six hundred cfs from two hundred. Because Colorado got a fairly good snowpack this season in that drainage up there so they probably have to make some room in the reservoir." But freezing temperatures and precipitation stifled any potential hatches and turned the fishing conditions into more of an endurance test than a comfortable and relaxed angling outing.

He had not yet fished Montana when we spoke, but had "heard a lot about it" and wanted to sometime.

Asked whether he had a special fishing friend, Weitz thought a few seconds before answering: "Well, I'm retired, so I tend to gravitate to other retired fishermen, but no, not particularly."

For him, fly fishing is "kind of a mix. I consider that I've always been a conservationist. But, you know, I'm not a serious fisherman, that's why I don't do as well as some other folks in the San Juan."

"Because when I retired and moved here then I took up bird watching -- which we don't call it that anymore, we call it birding -- and fly fishing. And I decided it's not as much urgency as the fish you catch, it's these places where neat looking birds and nice fish live."

In line with his dispassionate scientist's outlook, he does not think fly fishing imparts philosophical perspectives or life lessons. "It's a pleasurable, enjoyable pastime," he said.

Still, it is an important part of his life. "It's up there pretty high, he said. "I primarily read, anymore. I guess it's second or third. It's ahead of birding. I guess I'd have to say it's second."

His book selection is eclectic and includes both fiction and nonfiction. "I don't mind some shit-kicker westerns, interesting spy novels, and some of these historical novels are very interesting. . . . My nonfiction is primarily about World War II," he said.

Early history is also a favorite topic of his. "There's a guy named . . . Bernard Cornwell who wrote about the battle of Agincourt," Weitz said. "He writes primarily about the development of history and events. Well I just finished one that he wrote a while back and it started in the fourth century when the Vikings, or the Scandinavians, were wanting to move in and take over what are now the British Isles."

With more than seven thousand, seven hundred hours in his logbook, Weitz does miss flying. "Well, right now it's not a choice," he acknowledged. "If I had the choice I would still be flying, but I recognize that at my age I would need someone to be with me. So that was a different phase of my life and it was a full-time job, both of them. Both before I got into the astronaut business and while I was there. But no, I don't do those things anymore and I wanted to find something to spend some time on that was pleasurable and that's why birding and fly fishing came along."

But the man who spent nearly eight hundred hours orbiting the earth still had "THE RIGHT STUFF" for one more adventure. "I'm going to Alaska in August and we're going to fish the Kenai, because I never have," he said. "I'll be eighty-two years old and I don't travel well anymore. That's kind of my swan song out of the home area. . . . .We're going mainly for the trout and the char. Not so much for the salmon."

Chapter 19
Randy Wayne White:
Adventurer by the Book

It is no mystery how Randy Wayne White became one of the top selling genre writers in the United States -- talent, persistence, and hard work. White, a onetime charter fishing guide in southwest Florida who came to his true calling in an oblique way, is now a mini-industry, with interests in restaurants, sauces, and even a cookbook.

Wendy Webb, © Randy Wayne White

From modest beginnings, White, mostly through his own efforts, has come to fit the cliché "larger than life," a celebrity as well as an accomplished writer. A onetime high school athlete, his strapping physique and forthright demeanor fit the image of a former linebacker more than that of a literary maven.

White is a Midwestern native who grew up in Ohio and Iowa. But he did most of his early fishing in North Carolina, where he spent many summers and where his family has deep roots. He recalled those nascent bobber-and-worm angling outings with fondness.

"Growing up I fished with my mother, who was a superb fisherman," he said. "Pee Dee River, North Carolina. We'd use porcupine bobbers (made from the animal's quills), which is one of the most delightful ways to fish."

After high school, White assuaged his innate wanderlust with wide-ranging travels, settling in the early 1970s on Sanibel Island in southwest Florida. He worked at the Fort Myers News-Press – a daily newspaper -- and then became a fishing guide, docking his boat in Tarpon Bay and plying the waters of Pine Island Sound, San Carlos Bay, and the Gulf of Mexico with clients for thirteen years. His guiding exploits would bring him to fly fishing and eventually provide the nucleus of an enormously successful book series: the Doc Ford mysteries.

"I actually got interested in fly fishing – I got my captain's license in seventy-four so I was guiding part time," White recounted. "And one of my clients was a very fine fly fisherman. He came down to my boat with this strange get-up, a very long, willowy rod and Nautilus reel, as I recollect."

"At the time, among the people that I knew, the thought was that the water was too murky to fly fish (in the backwaters). I knew no one who fly fished, nor did any of the other guides, but I started going out. And I'll never forget on my first trip we were fishing by Marker 13A (Pine Island Sound) outside Tarpon Bay, across near

York Island. Just blind casting as we drifted, three to six feet of water, and a tarpon hit his fly and I thought he was going to have a heart attack, I almost did, too. Ike Hayes, I think he was, from New York. This was a long time ago, 1980."

"And the thinking at that time was that tarpon wouldn't hit a fly here because it was too murky," he repeated. But having seen evidence to the contrary, White set out to learn the new (to him) sport. "In Cape Coral there was a guy named Bruce Brubaker, who at that time was the world fly casting accuracy champion," he said. "You meet the most interesting people in southwest Florida. I contacted Bruce, he gave me some casting lessons, and I was never a great caster, but I did learn to cast left handed and right handed. Because if you're a fishing guide, most people are right handed, and you're better off throwing left."

"Anyway, I became an aficionado of the sport, largely because the people who I met as clients were just some terrific, classy, classy men, and women. And another common belief at that time was that the tarpon offshore, even if the water was clear, you couldn't land them because a fly rod didn't have enough lifting power." The guides along Florida's southwest coast had obviously not kept up with the exploits of Ted Williams, Lefty Kreh, Joe Brooks, Stu Apte, et al down in the Florida Keys.

White took the situation in hand to follow his own instincts. "In the early eighties I went to Glenn Pace's Tackle (in Fort Myers) and we talked about it," he said. "So he made for me an Ugly Stik fly rod and it was a 10-weight. And so I took Ike Hayes, late spring, we ran offshore and we were looking at acres of tarpon. Ike landed a tarpon in thirty feet of water."

All the guides "were aware of this unusual incident," White said. "And then it became a regular thing. We used a sink-tip line out there."

He has never been a fan of fishing tournaments. "I'm truly not a competitive person in terms of fishing," he said. "Although, ego is involved. I care about the clients. . . . All that bullshit, I can't bear it. I can't tolerate it. Fly casting to me, fly fishing, had a wonderful way to link me to the mastery of sports fishing. People say fly fishing is an art, well it's not, it's a craft. Fly *tying* might be an art. I like the subtleties of it, and I enjoyed the people; my clients, the fly fishing clients. As wonderful as all my clients were, fly fishermen were just a step above."

Although fly fishing held no competitive attraction for him, White had a more receptive opinion of casting competitions, even writing about one for one of his nonfiction books.

"It was held in Vail, Colorado, and it was at Silver Creek, it might have been called Silver Creek Fly Fishing. And I was invited out there. It was called something like the Vail International Fly Casting Championship. It was kind of tongue in cheek," he said. "One event was, we cast at nine holes of a golf course. You'd start at the tee, and then cast your fly line. It was a lot of fun. Another was you had to tie an Albright knot blindfolded. That was my event. There was a spawning run upriver, which I didn't do very well in. And there was accuracy. Anyway, I placed second. I won a beautiful little Abel fly reel."

It was during his guiding years that White also began writing for profit. Eventually he parlayed his penchant for visiting exotic locales into a lucrative career by traveling to and writing about the farthest corners of the world. This was participatory, first-person adventure travel journalism that paralleled the rise of Outside magazine, which eagerly underwrote his assignments to sometimes dangerous places and hair-raising experiences. Over several decades his travels have taken him from Sumatra to Central America, Africa to Australia, and many places in between. Collections of his adventure travel tales include *Batfishing in the Rainforest, The Sharks of Lake Nicaragua* and *Last Flight Out*. When we spoke he was in a deadline crunch following a trip to Guyana.

Simultaneously, White dived into the turbulent waters of fiction, publishing books under the names Randy Striker beginning in 1981and Carl Ramm in 1984. But it was his 1990 mystery *Sanibel Flats*, published under his own name, that catapulted him to the literary stratosphere. The book's two main characters, marine biologist Marion "Doc" Ford and his superannuated hippie pal, Tomlinson, have formed the foundation for one of the most successful literary franchises of recent decades.

The Doc Ford phenomenon is also reflected in the success of three eponymous themed restaurants throughout southwest Florida in which White is part owner. The eateries are hugely popular book signing venues for the author, who often heads out on nationwide promo tours.

White's self discipline and productivity are legendary; traits that have made him one of the country's most prolific authors, with more than forty published books. His fiction books are action stories, often set in exotic locales, and fraught with violence and local color. These are not novels of manners and cerebral maunderings. Occasionally, though, he does salt them with existential quips. In recent years his novels have consistently made it onto the New York Times Bestseller List. The American Independent Mystery Booksellers Association picked *Sanibel Flats* as one of the hundred favorite mysteries of the twentieth century.

White is modestly circumspect about one aspect of his apprenticeship in fly fishing. "You know, I really didn't start anything in this area," he said. "I want to be very careful not to take credit for something I didn't do, but what I told you about fly fishing was absolutely true."

He defers to other guides on the pioneering aspect of his southwest Florida saltwater forays. "I think Rick O'Bannon was a far better fly fisherman than I," he said. "I think the O'Bannon's -- Rick and Phil – were starting to do some fly fishing at that time. And the only reason I recall that is because I happened to pull into the old marina at Punta Rassa and Phil was there and I saw fly rods. . . . It might have been the early eighties."

When he stopped guiding, White passed on much – but not all -- of his fishing gear to his two sons. He still fly fishes and two months before this interview flew down with a couple of friends to the Bahamas to chase bonefish.

"We did great," he said. "I actually didn't plan on fishing. But I went out with Mark Futch (a friend from southwest Florida). On a real windy day the guide said, here, get your ass up here. So I got up there (on the bow) and started throwing into the wind and starting getting my loop right, started to get my loop contained, and, Christ, I caught a bunch of little bonefish. It was fun. . . . They ate like little piggies."

White lamented the fact that he seemed unable to make more time for a sport he loves. "I really have to change something. I write, always have, essentially seven days a week, that's the problem. The deadline obligations, correspondence, and charities. . . . I still have a fly rod rigged and ready and if I see tarpon down by the beach – which I often do in the fall, that's a phenomenon -- I'll go on down and more often than not I'll clip off the point of the hook and then just get a jump or a run."

Though almost all of his fly fishing has been in the salt, White has sampled freshwater. "I've done a little in Idaho and Colorado," he said. "And I enjoyed the subtleties of it. I wasn't very successful. I loved the way it smelled."

Though White cares deeply about the natural world, he refuses to be pigeonholed. "There are a number of so-called environmentalists that disagree that I'm an environmentalist," he said. "I travel so much that I'm all too aware that the first casualty of a failed economy is the environment. So I'm for free enterprise, particularly small business. I am less and less tolerant of the unthinking, blind, so-called environmental groups. . . . I like to think I'm a realist who appreciates the environment.

One thing he learned from the sport is, "There is a continuity, whatever pastime or vocation we choose we, in a sense, channel our predecessors. In regards to fly fishing, Ted Williams . . . Captain (Jimmie) Albright. Another thing it taught me. Women, in my experience, learn fly casting far easier and far more quickly than men. They don't overpower the rod and they listen to what you say."

Many of us have a number one fishing buddy and White is no exception. "My favorite all-time fishing companion is (fellow author) Peter Matthiessen. In fact, Pete just came down a month or two ago, and we did have three wonderful days. He came down and Bill Bishop (guide, outdoor writer, and angling artist) -- he is absolutely superb -- he took Peter and me out. It was windy, but Peter still had a couple of shots at big fish."

These days he has taken up another aquatic pastime, also partly centered around fish. "I paddle board," he said. "It's very intimate, I see a lot of fish. I've seen more bull sharks than I've ever seen in my life." Because of their ferocity and penchant for hunting in packs, bull sharks are the bane of tarpon fishermen's endeavors and have a well-earned reputation as one of the oceans' most dangerous predators for humans. One time White was videoing a large one swimming around his board when he slipped and fell on top of it, causing it to shoot away like a torpedo. Having been peripherally acquainted with him for nearly twenty years – observing the way he carries himself, his physical bulk, his confident mien – I was not surprised at the shark's reaction.

Chapter 20
Jack Ohman:
Artist With Pen and Fly

Jack Ohman, editorial cartoonist for the Sacramento Bee newspaper and considered one of the top artists in his field, wields his drawing pen with a satirical wit as sharp as a newly filed hook. The same ironic, jabbing style comes to the fore in conversation. It is implicit to his opinions, ideas, and speech patterns and is employed with impartiality on friends and acquaintances, national and world events, and his own foibles.

Jack Ohman

As is the case with many people with outstanding natural talent and relentless drive, his career took off early. At seventeen he was working at the University of Minnesota student newspaper and by nineteen was he was the youngest cartoonist ever to be nationally syndicated. At the time this chapter was written his work was syndicated and appearing in more than three hundred newspapers. His long list of honors and awards includes The 2009 Robert F. Kennedy Journalism Award, the 1995 Thomas Nast Award, and the 2010 Society of Professional Journalists Award. In addition he has authored and/or illustrated ten books on politics, journalism, and fly fishing. One of the best known is his 2009 autobiographical work *Angler Management,* which is replete with laugh-out-loud quips and illustrations as well as serious quasi-existentialist observations drawn from his life and times and ranging from the absurd to the deeply moving.

Fishing, especially fly fishing, has been part of Ohman's life for the better part of half a century. And yet he cuts himself no slack. Given his extensive fly fishing experience and success, however, one suspects that his self-critical comments are partly hyper modesty and sand-bagging.

"I was probably six when I was exposed to fly fishing and thirty-nine when I learned to fly fish," he said. "I had a thirty-three year experimentation window."

As a young boy in Marquette, Michigan, he "did a lot of worm and bobber fishing" with his dad. . . . "Then we moved to D.C. and there was a lot of opportunity for that. So I managed to find some creek fishing around there . . . for carp, bullhead, things like that."

"And then we moved to Minnesota and I got very interested in bass fishing and after a while I got very interested in popper fishing and fly fishing for crappies and bass (at fourteen)," he said. "And having had the endless outdoor media fascist power structure tell me that trout were better than bass, I then started investigating fishing for trout."

"There was a very good river that was by the Twin Cities, it's called the Kinnikinnic. So I had a couple friends who were my age who were way down the road on this. I mean they understood tippet material and were excellent fly tiers and were matching hatches and they had Swisher/Richards in their backpack. I was just using eight-pound monofilament for leaders and so I would see them catch lots of fish and I would get the very, very odd accidental fish.

"I had a Shakespeare Wonder Rod and a Pfleuger Medalist. But as I got a little more competent, I figured out leaders and things like that and how to tie the knots, right." During this time, Ohman said, "I kind of did just the basic nymph fishing. I was just very almost clueless about dry fly fishing and drift.

"I liked it but I just couldn't take the time to do it right. I wasn't very successful. I caught fish by accident." He described himself as being "very ADD," adding however, "I don't know if I am clinically. . . . I am driven and active. What happens is when I get hyper focused on something, then I *do* learn it."

With fly fishing, this zeroing in took place when he moved to the Northwest in 1983 to work for The Oregonian newspaper, in Portland. "I got very focused on it. I met a bunch of older guys and they kind of took me another way. . . . Two guys in particular were very much my mentors," he said. "One was a nymph fisherman and the other was just very avid with things that happened in fly fishing. Jim Ramsey was the dry fly fisherman and Dick Thomas was the nymph guy. Between watching them – and they're still alive and they're in their late seventies and eighties now," he said.

Ohman is very clear about the priority of fly fishing in his life. "I wrote in my book (*Angler Management*) that I was amazed how many major life decisions I have made that were based only on fly fishing," he said. "You know, we can't live there, there is no trout fishing. Or, I want to buy a beach house but I need to know that there is a stream that I can walk to. Or making sure that my ex-wife was okay with fly fishing. Many vacations were structured around, they want to this and this and this, then I need to be able to get to fly fishing within half an hour or an hour. So that was a disaster. When I think it through I think it drove my ex-wife crazy."

His obsession also affected major career choices. "I did not take a job on the Seattle Times because I felt that it would be too far to drive for basic, low-end trout fishing. . . . I was told that and I was in shock," he said. "Because it's all about salmon in Seattle. And this was a damn good job. . . . But, I mean, if there had been fly fishing within an hour of Seattle or two hours, I probably would have been on board, but it was four. They said, ah you gotta drive over to Wenatchee. I was like, screw that."

"There are many, many things I did in my life when I thought about that. And now, mid-career, would I make a change, where would that be, what would the fishing situation be?" he asked.

Even Portland had its limitations, he conceded. "There are little pockets, there are private lakes, and maybe some streams where you might be able to jerk a trout out, or two. There is some cutthroat fishing up in the Coast Range. . . . Your closest good, reliable river is the Deschutes and that's two hours."

At the time this chapter was written, he had been at the Bee only a few months and was considering the Owens, the Sacramento, and smaller waters within two hours' drive. Pondering the possibilities, he waxed nostalgic for the waters of his youth.

"If you live in Marquette, Michigan, when I did when I was a kid . . . you can go to the Chalkley, that's what, ten, twenty minutes, you can go to the Dead, that's twenty minutes," he said. "You can go fish the Carp, that's down the street. I would go fish in the Carp as a fourteen-year-old and you would catch brookies, you would catch browns, you would catch rainbows. They were not big, but they were in there and it was fun. And there wasn't any pressure

"In Minnesota, my God, well I lived in a suburb and they were having bass tournaments down at this lake," he said." I mean, guys were getting six-, seven-, eight-pound bass out of there!"

Looking back, Ohman regards his father as a disappointment to his fly fishing aspirations. "He tried to take it up and he never got anywhere with it," he said. He was very much a Rapala guy. He didn't really do enough of it. . . . He was a very accomplished scientist for the U.S. Forest Service. So he was quite busy, and as he got older he got busier. So he wasn't doing a 'Big Two-Hearted River' thing. And, wow, that's what I wanted. I wanted: 'Big Two-Hearted River.' "

But though he recalled his father as sometimes too tough and emotionally distant, he felt a powerful filial tenderness and took care of him for the last four years of his life, performing some of the most intimate and unpleasant tasks and procedures, such as changing his catheters.

"My hero was – I never met him -- Robert Traver," he said. "And he lived right by us. He's listed in our 1968 phone book. In Deer Park (Michigan). His real name was John Voelker." Traver, ne Voelker, wrote the best selling murder mystery *Anatomy of a Murder,* as well as numerous fly fishing books.

Despite his fame and accomplishments, Ohman harbors no grandiose fly fishing aspirations. In fact, his preferences tend toward the acronym KISS (keep it simple stupid).

"My favorite type of fly fishing would be some kind of small stream, big rock, not heavy wading environment where maybe I was wearing hip boots and I was hitting some good brook trout," he said. "You know, like nine to twelve. . . . I hate putting on my waders, I hate standing out in the water, I hate fighting the current. . . . I can't stand to go steelheading. It's too time consuming and too much work."

Like many of us, Ohman has a favorite fly. "It's called a Deerhair Spider Emerger," he revealed. "I describe it in *Angler Management* in detail. It is kind of a Humpy without color. And it is dynamite. It works as a caddis, it works as a blue-wing olive, it's a good attractor fly, it's a good all-around, you know, it's brown and gray. It's a good searching fly and it floats like hell. . . . It's from an old timer fly shop in Sisters (Oregon)."

Ohman thought a moment before evaluating his own skills. "I consider myself a highly competent high "B" fly fisherman," he ventured. "I'm a good caster, I tie my own flies, they're fine and they work, they're not works of art. But I can tie a Clark Stone and a Deer Hair Spider Emerger and pretty much anything I would need to tie. I don't know if that puts me in the A group or not."

When we talked, Ohman pondered his fly fishing future in light of the fact that his children had grown up and moved away. "I'm a very busy person, unfortunately, and there are always places I know I should be going to and now my last kid is going to college," he said. "So I am faced with the very real possibility that I'm going to have vast stretches of unstructured time, number one, and, number two, that I am not going to live forever. So I've been thinking more about, you know, you should go fish the Pan and you should go fish the Clark's Fork."

His daughter had recently started graduate school at the University of Montana. "I'm hoping we'll have a little five-year interregnum there where I can really get to know that area," he said.

As far as a favorite river, Ohman hedged in his answer. "Well if I were on a float trip on the Deschutes that would be great. The Deschutes has such powerful fish and they've got good opportunities to hit eighteens every day. . . . And I love going up to Idaho and fishing the North Fork of the Clearwater and sometimes it can just be, you know, ridiculous." He lamented the fact that his fly fishing time had shrunk. "In my prime I was doing thirty, forty (days a year) and I was really fighting for that. And now I'm probably only doing ten, fifteen, twenty maybe. No more than twenty-five.

The MacKenzie and the Crooked River have been frequent spring-summer destinations for Ohman. In the fall he sometimes heads to Ketchum, Idaho, where he fishes mainly the Big Wood. Like many literary pilgrims, he once made it a point to visit Ernest Hemingway's grave in the cemetery outside town. "I put a penny on it along with the fourteen thousand other people who put a penny on it," he said.

Though he comes across as straightforward, practical angler, he did evince a spiritual perspective. "You can be on the river and you can be looking down on it and you can see the river and you can see the bugs coming off and you can see the trout coming up and you can see the vast deadness around it, basically. It's like a full illustration of how the universe works. We're born, we die, there is regeneration, it keeps moving, it's beautiful, it's scary, you could die while doing it, it's barren, it's lush, it's everything. I think if people are open to being taught, it has a lot of lessons."

He lamented the young generation of fly fishers' lack of historical and literary perspective about the sport and their focus on technical expertise. For him, this is only part of the picture. "I can't tie a whip finish but I know who Theodore Gordon is," he said.

Ohman puts fly fishermen into two categories: the "predator type" and the "experience fly fisherman." He includes himself in the latter category. "I kind of visualize the predator fly fishermen are counting, or they're secretly forgetting to mash their barbs," he said. "They WANT to kill a fish. They're like, I got seventeen, how many have you got? I'm more like, wow, I turned an awesome fish. And I don't know what to ascribe that to."

He also sees the sport from a creative perspective. "I love the aesthetics of it," he said. "I mean, as an artist, empirically, the older I've gotten the more I appreciate all the little things of fly fishing that don't involve gear collection. I marvel at the mechanics of it and I marvel at the intricacy and the absurdity of the concept of fishing a fly, where this is made out of animals and metal, and it's hard to get the metal, it's all so precise, and yet a lot of people know, I think, a scroungier looking fly works better than a perfectly tied fly. . . . It's like the abstract painting versus the paint by numbers painting."

"I would rank fly fishing number two," Ohman said of his top free time pursuits. It is closely followed by cycling. Number one? " Being with women," he answered coyly, with no hint of irony. "Notice how I phrased it. That would definitely be my default activity."

For many of us, the quietude of fly fishing is implicit to our love of the sport. On this point Ohman is an iconoclast: He loves to listen to music while fly fishing, especially "awe inspiring classic 1940s Big Band music." One can imagine Tommy Dorsey and Glenn Miller blasting through his I-Pod ear buds as he plays a trout.

Asked about a dream trip, he eschewed the exotic and waxed nostalgic. "I would like to go back to Marquette, Michigan, and fish with my dad," he said, with a catch in his throat, wistful, like many of us, about memories of time spent on the water with people we have loved.

Chapter 21
Jeff Fisher:
Gridirons and Gravel Bars

When Jeff Fisher was not pushing his Los Angeles Rams players to reach their peak playing potential, he might be found casting a fly rod on one of his favorite trout streams. Fisher, a longtime savvy, hard-driving NFL coach and former star high school, college, and pro football player, also loves the radically dissimilar ambiance of the "quiet sport." In speaking with him it quickly became clear that both pursuits occupy large portions of his life.

Jeff Fisher

Born in Culver City, California, Fisher first made his mark in football as a high school All-American at Woodland Hills' Taft High School. He later became a star at the University of Southern California, playing on the Trojans' 1978 national championship team. Though he had been a wide receiver in high school, at USC he was moved to the defense as a cornerback but also filled in on returns. In addition to his on-field accomplishments, in 1980 he was named a Pac-10 all-academic pick.

In 1981 he joined the Chicago Bears, playing four years as a cornerback and punt returner. With the Bears he set a team record for punt return yards with five hundred and nine yards in the 1981 season. That same year he had the Bears' longest punt return in four decades with an eighty-eight yard touchdown run. His playing career was cut short in 1985 by an injured ankle that came only two years after he had broken his leg. While out of action Fisher was picked to help Bears defensive coordinator Buddy Ryan. The next year Ryan took over the top job at the Philadelphia Eagles and took Fisher with him as defensive backs coach. In 1988 the Eagles made him defensive coordinator.

Fisher's coaching internships continued until 1994, when he was named to replace fired Houston Oilers head coach Jack Pardee. When the Oilers left Houston for Memphis, Fisher moved with them. After another move, to Nashville, and a team name change, to the Tennessee Titans in 1999, he reached a period of comparative job stability for the next twelve years.

It was during the Titan years that Fisher established his reputation as one of the NFL's coaching greats, leading the team to multiple playoff appearances, including Super Bowl XXXIV and two AFC Championship Games. His teams were known for their hard-nosed, aggressive play, especially in rushing defense and offensive running totals. After a disappointing 6-10 season in 2010, partly occasioned by quarterback troubles, the Titans let Fisher go.

Sometimes the tranquility of fly fishing can be a refuge from the hyper-competitive, dog-eat-dog world of professional sports. When Fisher and the Tennessee Titans parted ways in January 2011 he was not shattered. In a tone of bonhomie – likely boosted by a healthy severance package -- he told reporters, "I'm going to take the next year off, head to Montana and do some fly fishing and backpacking!"

A year after leaving Nashville he took over as head coach for the then St. Louis Rams and in 2012 helped put five more games in the win column than the previous year's team. When this chapter was written, Fisher's NFL career coaching record totals were 149-128-1, or .539 percent. His tenure with the Oilers/Titans lasted sixteen years, the longest one-team span among active coaches.

In spring 2013, in a curious footnote in the wake of his Tennessee departure, Vince Young, a former Titans quarterback under Fisher, issued a letter of apology to his ex-coach. Young expressed regret for actions that likely damaged Fisher's Tennessee legacy and praised him for "trying to make me become one of those types of leaders on the team, a successful quarterback." He admitted he had been "immature and not paying attention and not listening, and taking my frustration out on a lot of people."

When we spoke, Fisher was putting in long days running spring camp workouts, evaluating rookies, and trying to get a handle on the upcoming season roster. And dreaming of Montana.

Fisher first used a fly rod as a little boy in waters near his southern California home and farther afield, in the Sierra Nevada Mountains. "When Dad put a fly rod into my hand I was eight or nine," he said. But in a not radically atypical quirk of method – think Nick Adams drifting live grasshoppers in "Big Two-hearted River" – there were no flies involved. "Dad loves to bait-fish with a fly rod," Fisher explained, chuckling.

Despite the sometimes hectic lifestyle of a star athlete in high school and college, Fisher still made time for occasional fly fishing.

"I'd get up into, whether it was the Sierras or streams outside Los Angeles . . . above Bishop (near the Nevada border), in that area," he said.

It was the early 1990s, Fisher said, when he began focusing in on fly fishing and making it a personal major pastime. Since then he has traveled far and wide, trekking to British Columbia's White River for huge bull trout and to Guatemala for sailfish. He also "chased some baby tarpon around Cancun (Mexico)," and in 2004 traveled to far southern Chile, making forays to remote Andean trout rivers "where no one had ever fished." But his fly fishing pole star is and has long been Big Sky Country.

Fisher has cast many miles of Montana's storied trout waters. He has floated the South Fork of the Flathead in northwest Montana, and regularly fishes in Yellowstone National Park. "I love the Gibbon," he said. And the grayling of Flathead National Forest's Handkerchief Lake intrigue him. But the love of his angling life is the Madison, where his family's cabin on Hebgen Lake allows him to escape from the hurly burly of professional football.

Fisher's cabin is ideally located to fish a variety of waters. "We can do the Henry's Fork in the morning and float a reasonable float on the Madison in the afternoon and then go over to the Jefferson for the evening hatch," he said.

In both his profession and his avocation, Fisher has made a conscious effort to give back. He was one of the strongest proponents for the NFL rule change that banned runners from lowering their heads to hit tacklers with the tops of their helmets. The new rule, enacted in spring 2013, was intended to reduce the number and severity of injuries, especially traumatic brain injuries. Fisher's love of the game prompted him to call the change "a very important step in our efforts to emphasize players' safety" and "a huge victory for the National Football League. . . . We've lost the shoulder in the game," he said, "let's bring it back."

On the fly fishing side, he joined Craig and Jackie Matthews' crusade to shortstop development and preserve public access to miles of the Madison River up- and downstream from the legendary Three Dollar Bridge. The Matthews, owners of Blue Ribbon Flies in West Yellowstone, Montana, spearheaded the movement that in 2002 culminated in Montana Fish, Wildlife and Parks' taking over stewardship of the stretch with a promise that "this property would forever be preserved and open to the public." Through working together on the campaign, Fisher said, "I got to be good friends with Craig."

Fisher has also been active in fundraising and promotion for the Wounded Warriors Project, including a 2011 Africa trip to climb Mount Kilimanjaro with four injured veterans and several other NFL figures. His annual Coach Fisher & Friends Celebrity Softball Game, held under the aegis of the Rams organization, also raises funds for WWP and a handful of other charity groups.

Like most highly successful people, Fisher loves his job. "I'm very fortunate to be doing what I'm doing," he said. But though it is impossible to imagine him grousing about the time demands and pressures of big-time sports, he does value his down time and spends most of it outdoors. "I enjoy bow hunting," he said. "Not so much with a rifle." Throughout our conversation, however, he left no doubt about where fly fishing ranks: "It's number one."

Fisher loves the wild and exotic, but also the everyday hometown joys of the sport. On his farm outside Nashville is a four-acre pond that he stocks with trout for backyard fun with family and friends. When it comes to the coach's favorite water, the Madison wins hands down.

And he does appreciate the lessons learned in fly fishing. One, he said, is the importance of a conservation ethos, including basic concepts, such as taking the time to be gentle with the fish when releasing them, a practice he said comes with angling success.

Gentleness, he said, "Is in contrast with what we do here (at training camp) in a high contact sport."

Other aspects of Fisher's thoughtful conservation philosophy include activism, such as the Three Dollar Bridge crusade, and just speaking up against harmful and senseless practices."There is a creek about an hour and a half from the cabin," he said. . . . "Fish and game is killing it off to restore it to its 'natural' state." Fisher knew his opposition would likely not stop the seemingly ill-advised project, but made his opinion known anyway.

Another valuable lesson from fly fishing, he said, is "the importance of getting away with friends and family." He and his wife and three kids have spent many happy weeks at Hebgen Lake.

Fisher sees no carry-over from his NFL persona to the man who wades and drifts the Madison. On the water, the hard-driving football strategist who focuses on his team's hammering opponents into submission disappears. The fierce competitor transforms into a patient and relaxed angler exuding Zen-like tranquility. "I don't mind casting to the same fish for an hour, in the same spot," he said. It is a comment not many other fly fishers would make.

There is no room for competitiveness in Fisher's angling world view. In a nod to his son Brandon's skill with a fly rod he acknowledged with a chuckle that, "Anyway, if competition is involved I'm going to lose to my son." Brandon Fisher, who studied and played football at the University of Montana in Missoula, also used his Big Sky Country academic sojourn to become a top-notch fly fisher; so good that his best fishing buddy, his dad, called him "my mentor."

Brandon, who was twenty-six when this chapter was written, had begun working for Fisher as assistant secondary coach with the Rams. However, his father said only half kiddingly, "He'd leave the business (football) and go fly fishing," if he got the chance.

It is an outlook that one is sure the coach understands very well.*

*Coach Jeff Fisher left the L.A. Rams in 2016, while this book was in final preparation.

Index

Research Sources

DISCovering U.S. History on GaleNet

wikipedia.org

Lazy B: Growing up on a Cattle Ranch in the American Southwest, by Sandra Day O'Connor and H. Alan Day

The Boston Globe, "Wade Boggs: 2005 Hall of Fame Inductee: Nothing Average About Five-Time Batting Champ," By Dan Shaughnessy, July 31, 2005

The Tampa Tribune, "The Tampa Years -- A Star in The Making," By Joe Henderson, Jul 29, 2005

Ernest Hemingway: A Life Story, by Carlos Baker, Charles Scribner's Sons, © 1969

latimes.com/features/lifestyle/

jsc.nasa.gov/Bios

pro-football-reference.com

espn.go.com

blue-ribbon-flies.com

history.nasa.gov

astronautscholarship.org

azgfd.gov

prweb.com

National Baseball Hall of Fame

National Aeronautics and Space Administration

cfr.org

businessweek.com

Michael P. Johnson, Master's Thesis, University of North Texas: Skylab, the Human Side of a Scientific Mission, 2007

biography.com

Cornell Chronicle, Oct. 24, 2007

CPSIA information can be obtained
at www.ICGtesting.com
Printed in the USA
LVOW06*0217100817

544482LV00036B/238/P